LAST WORDS

T0163302

LAST WORDS

STORIES

HUGH GRAHAM

EXILE
editions

Library and Archives Canada Cataloguing in Publication

Graham, Hugh, 1951-, author
Last words : stories / Hugh Graham.

Issued in print and electronic formats.
ISBN 978-1-55096-486-8 (paperback).--ISBN 978-1-55096-487-5 (epub).
--ISBN 978-1-55096-488-2 (mobi).--ISBN 978-1-55096-489-9 (pdf)

I. Title

PS8563.R3165L37 2015   C813'.6   C2015-903601-1
                                               C2015-903602-X

Copyright © Hugh Graham, 2015

Design and Composition by Mishi Uroboros
Typeset in Big Caslon and Hellas Fun fonts at Moons of Jupiter Studios

Published by Exile Editions Ltd ~ www.ExileEditions.com
144483 Southgate Road 14 – GD, Holstein, Ontario, N0G 2A0
Printed and Bound in Canada in 2015, by Marquis Books

We gratefully acknowledge, for their support toward our publishing
activities, the Canada Council for the Arts, the Government of Canada
through the Canada Book Fund, the Ontario Arts Council,
and the Ontario Media Development Corporation.

The use of any part of this publication, reproduced, transmitted in any
form or by any means, electronic, mechanical, photocopying, recording,
or otherwise stored in a retrieval system, without the expressed written
consent of the publisher (info@exileeditions.com) is an infringement of
the copyright law. For photocopy and/or other reproductive copying,
a license from Access Copyright (800 893 5777) must be obtained.

Canadian sales: The Canadian Manda Group, 664 Annette Street,
Toronto ON M6S 2C8 www.mandagroup.com 416 516 0911

North American and International Distribution, and U.S. Sales:
Independent Publishers Group, 814 North Franklin Street,
Chicago IL 60610   www.ipgbook.com   toll free: 1 800 888 4741

TO MARIA, JESSICA AND SAM.

EXT TO LAST

Last had begun to put his final hopes in Ariade, a woman whom he'd observed in the Luxembourg Gardens. Around one, most afternoons, she would sit at the same table tanning her legs, which she put up on the opposite chair. He would take the next table, where he usually read. Eventually he began to chat. She spoke indifferently, amused, her eyes closed, her face turned to the sun. If she were reading, she spoke without taking her eyes off her book. She would have been aware of a man who looked a little dishevelled, anonymous, a life in transit. He was careful to leave long silences so she could read.

Occasionally Last arrived when it was cloudy and she was not there. It was clear that she came only for the sun, not for him. Still, Last came to hope for sunny days. As a rule, he disliked sunny days which had always meant the workaday world and its expectations. Last preferred a lowering sky, or fog; a sense of things not being normal, of something impending.

When it was sunny, in the Luxembourg, Ariade finally began to ask him the odd question about himself. Then she would smoke a cigarette in silence. Then he would ask her a question. She was finishing her doctoral thesis on Syrian predecessors to the Bogomils and worked the early morning shift at a nearby all-night pharmacy. She was dark and slender, elegant. She wore light loose shifts and minimal sandals. On a crowded Sunday, when she allowed someone to take the opposite chair, she raised her legs and crossed her feet on Last's knee.

That night Last looked into the mirror and wondered if it was possible any longer to love someone like himself. At forty-nine he still had brownish hair, which, like the eyes behind the silver-rimmed glasses, was devoid of lustre. His hair was a thatch and he was thin. He looked winded, as if he'd been chased through a hailstorm; at least he had the patina of some-one who had lived. If unsuccessful, he was intelligent. If facing eventual poverty, he dressed well. The less money he had, the more possessions he gave up, the more often he had his clothes dry-cleaned and his shoes polished. He was always clean.

The following morning, as Last went out past the hotel reception, the manager announced loudly that he had no mail. Last had never had any mail since he'd been in France. Still, the manager, whose name was Henri, seemed to take pleasure in announcing it. Last even wondered if he knew about Ariade and the sunny days, since Henri had expatiated with cheerful condescension about a band of bad weather that approached France from Les Hébrides. Last had once liked Henri, who used the philosophy from his doctorate at the Sorbonne as a pursuit, not a career. Last had respected this; it addressed his own problem of getting through the day, which had become his chief problem.

He lived in a sort of mindless desperation. Continually, he had to leave wherever he was for somewhere else. He left the silence of his hotel every morning for the noise of a café, abandoned the anomie of the café for another café; that café for the brightness of the Luxembourg Gardens; the ruthlessness in the high afternoon sun in the Luxembourg for the cool solitude of the hotel room. The terrible late afternoon light in his room for the early dusk in the street. Wakefulness for sleep; the torments of sleep for the dreamless anxiety of wakefulness. In the evenings he smoked his single cigarette and drank, sometimes until he was drunk. And so on. He sought a calm centre which he never found. He sought stasis, yet when he found it, discovered that death lurked there. This was partly why he had left Toronto; in Paris it pursued him block to block. The narcotic which sustained him was reading. But he couldn't concentrate.

Even the idea of sightseeing filled him with boredom, sometimes rage. As he walked through the Sixtième and the Septième the following morning for his usual coffee, he reflected that he had never visited its great time-eaten monuments: St. Sulpice, the Odéon, St. Germain des Prés, Les Invalides. On the contrary, as early as his youth, he had become a connoisseur of the ugly, the blighted, the meaningless, the chaotic and the transitory. Humanity *décolleté*. It was behind the high-rises and freeways, the bleak industrial zones of Casablanca and Toronto that the great tidal flats of humanity and its history were exposed; in fragments of speech; in corruptions of names, in tribal peoples in apartment blocks; in adulterated vestiges of traditional cooking in fly-ridden restaurants. The final murmurs of individual humanity drowning in the very mass into which it was being transformed. Whereas if you went inside St. Sulpice, you would feel nothing. Once, after being stood up by a woman at a restaurant, he forced himself to go into the church of Les Invalides. Napoleon's battle flags hung high along the apse in a vaporous, meaningless, necromancy.

Last arrived at the café Mariem. He was having his coffee and reading the *Herald Tribune* when he became aware of someone sitting next to him, making noise with a newspaper. It was an American, perhaps forty, over six feet with acne scarring and glasses who had taken the next table though the terrace was empty. He was dressed in khaki chinos, Hush Puppies and white socks. He drank his coffee loudly and kept shaking out his newspaper. Last was about to move away when the American suddenly laughed and pointed to an editorial.

"Californian wines are threatening French wine exports. Unbelievable."

"Why?" Last said.

"It's all this stuff with France standing alone in their foreign policy on the war in Iraq. They're threatened. I think they're just playing the big *difference* card."

His name was Howard. He worked in the economics section at the American Embassy. Last asked what that meant. Howard said, "Beats me. A title looking for a job ... You know, I deal US investment in France, French exports. I'm bored, frankly. If somebody said, 'Where's your life going?' I'd say I honestly don't know."

Last sensed a rapport. They chatted about the French, about Americans and so on.

"What do you do?" Howard asked.

The question was bound to come, the answer many times rehearsed. "Taking time off," Last said. He added something vague about being an editor, conveyed a pensive existence. The truth was, he lived in a nightmare on dwindling savings brought from Canada.

"You sit in the cafés," Howard said. "That's fantastic. All day in the cafés. Wow."

Howard got up to go, and turned: "You usually here round now?"

Last said that he usually was.

"I'll probably see you. I've started running in the mornings. I pass by here."

Last liked Howard mostly because he was not at all like Last: Howard was friendly, up-front, open.

Last watched Howard cross the street and break into an athletic jog. He reflected that there were now two people he liked: Ariade and Howard. Though they didn't know one another, Last paired them in his mind; they seemed to give a dimension to things that wasn't there before. There was a sense of something happening.

A week later, in the Luxembourg, Ariade lay back in her chair, her skirt hiked up, her legs stretched out to the sun with one arm lying across Last's arm, which rested on the arm of his chair.

The next morning he was at the café Mariem again, reading the *Guardian* without taking any of it in.

"Hey, John!" Howard said and then sat down beside him. Howard was wearing shorts and a sweatband. The waiter arrived and they ordered. They talked about the war in Iraq. Last conveyed what he said was an eccentric but plausible explanation of the French position while Howard cleaned his glasses.

"That's weird. Where did that come from?"

"It was an editorial and some other stuff. I can't remember." It had come from Henri at the hotel.

In a while Howard was reflecting that he loved his wife but the prospect of separation had arisen. How would he fill his time alone? He was fascinated at how Last managed. With a lot of effort Last managed to make it sound interesting. Then Howard looked at his watch and said, "I gotta go. Ah, I think on Saturday, Cathy and I are having a few people over for a barbecue, I don't know if you're interested." Last took Howard's number, gave him the number of his hotel phone. Last had neither email nor cell phone. He knew no one.

"I'll have to see what's happening," Last said.

On Wednesday evening, Last and Ariade left the Luxembourg and saw a science-fiction movie about a penitentiary system without end. "It's sort of like life, I guess," Last said as they left. *"C'est tout à fait Gnostique,"* she said. Ariade took joyous flight in recondite references. She had spoken of some town planning as *"tout à fait Buddhiste."* Everything was *"tout à fait."* Her tan had intensified; he had felt the golden warmth of her arm against his throughout the movie.

On Saturday, Last set out for Howard's barbecue. Howard and Cathy Juarez lived in a house once owned by Napoleon's Marshal Duroc, now leased by Washington from the French. Cathy, a pert, scrubbed, Midwestern woman, led Last down a marble corridor, across Afghan carpets and into a glass-doored rococo salon heavy with mouldings, a Louis XVI fireplace and golden candle brackets. The furniture was arranged around a television and Sony PlayStation II. There was a red plastic tricycle shaped like a spaceship, a big yellow plastic duck on wheels, a toy rocket launcher and Masters of the Universe figures scattered on the rug with spilled cereal. On a Louis XVI commode, under a huge mirror whose frame featured a gilded Dido and Aeneas, stood a crowd of golf and softball trophies. The television was on. Cathy took Last through the doors into a stone courtyard trimmed with hedges and topiary. Most of the guests were Americans, among them a few French men and women who talked in forced, liberated Texan guffaws.

Howard greeted Last briefly and introduced him to several other people around one of two huge smoking barbecues. Last chatted with a few of them then spent the rest of the time standing near the topiary with his wine as thoughts wound, like a tangle of wire, deeper into his past. Since childhood, he had avoided joining anything, perhaps to hang on to a rigorous sense of who he was. Now he had long known who he was but was left with nothing but a sense of his utter worthlessness. When he looked up, the light had changed and many of the guests had left. He said goodbye to Cathy and Howard and went to the front door. Howard ran up and stopped him, apologized for getting caught up and invited him for dinner the following week.

Last thought it strange. But a few nights later he came again and places for three were set around the end of the dining room table. A two-year-old girl and a six-year-old boy played in the salon. An elderly maid and a young white-coated servant brought in *poulet chasseur*. Cathy began talking about Paris. In a while, the couple was showing an interest in Last and in his life that surprised him. Afterward, Cathy asked, "Do you have friends in Paris?" She said it in a sighing, emotional voice, as she said many things.

"Oh yeah, I know the odd...denizen," he said, and laughed. He didn't want to bring up Ariade, the only person he knew. He feared he was falling in love with her. He put it out of his mind. Cathy's eyes were filled with tears; somehow Last had painted a picture of stoic solitude, unspoken tragedy.

The following Sunday he came for a light lunch and they talked about some American movie stars living in Paris. By the third time, an evening when he came for drinks, a clear bond had begun to develop. The diplomatic world, Last thought, must be extremely lonely. Over a Wednesday night drink in a café, Cathy expressed fascination with Last's apparent "inner life," his solitude. He finally revealed that he had once been a poet and an editor. The image effortlessly emerged: the life without attachments; an enigmatic past in Toronto; a literary background, the absence of any definite occupation, the stoical maintenance of sanity by the fragile thread of routine. Howard gazed at him, smoking a cigar; Cathy seemed deeply moved. He could not remember when he had felt so easily understood.

Cathy went off to visit friends. Back at the house, Howard and Last sat down in the salon and had a drink. Howard swirled his wine in his glass and looked at the floor. He leaned forward, long and lumbering as a crane, and took a cigar out of a humidor. He offered one to Last. Last accepted.

Howard inhaled, exhaled a volume of blue smoke.

"I lied to you," he said.

"Lied?"

"Well, yes and no. My title and papers say I'm in the economics section. I'm actually in intelligence. CIA. Chief of station."

The work, apparently, was frustrating. Klenauwitz, a US Defense Department official, would be attending an honourary dinner at a restaurant in Rue Odéon with French-Jewish community leaders. The dinner was a prime target for terrorists. The Defense Department supplied the security for its official but the French were supposed to secure the location. Howard went on in some detail.

Trying to follow, Last said, "So the French, out of, I guess, obstinacy, aren't giving the security you need. Is it because the Paris Jewish community supported the US occupation of Iraq? And the French don't?"

"You got it," Howard said. "In fact, we know that there's an Algerian sleeper cell in Paris linked to al-Qaeda and they're following our movements. Twice Defense has had to change the locale of the dinner and we're almost sure the guy who's been casing these restaurants is an Algerian called Ali Hamadi. So now Defense has booked a place up in the Quinzième. I wanted to do surveillance but the State Department's saying no, it's a French responsibility."

Last realized he had read about the inter-agency rivalry, the excessive reliance on technology, the lack of assets on the ground.

"So I guess your hands are tied as far as surveillance is concerned," Last said.

"If I want it, I've got to do it under the table."

Last imagined the Paris underworld.

"What sort of terrorism?" Last said.

"Well, an attack on the restaurant. Possibly a suicide bombing," Howard said.

Last wondered what solution Howard could possibly find for such an intractable situation. What sorts of shady people would he have to deal with? Doubtless, the desperate, the exploitable.

Last found a bar-café called the Metronome up in the Quinzième on Rue Parterre. It had a clear view of the two streets that met at Chez Suzy, the Defense Department's latest choice of restaurant. He had arrived at eight and now had the *Herald Tribune* out on the table. He would be there for nine hours. At two hundred US per day for a week or two it would stave off eventual penury. Another asset would spell him off at night.

Howard had shown him photographs taken from surveillance. Grubby and obscure, they caught Ali Hamadi, a short and burly balding man of about forty with a trimmed moustache and a blunt aquiline nose in a sweat suit; in a leather jacket; getting into an Audi, going down the Metro. Within a brief time of seeing Hamadi, Last was to phone, always from a pay phone. To Last it had seemed the perfect job but when Howard had warned him that it was work, you couldn't just sit around reading all the time, Last had nearly backed out.

By eleven in the morning, it was getting even harder than he had thought. He sneaked a glance at the *Tribune* then back at the streets around Chez Suzy. Finally he was doing something. Something for human life. He had never done anything for human life. And now there was Ariade as well. He wondered how a new love might fit into a year-long routine of sitting in cafés reading the *Herald Tribune*, the *New York Review of Books*, the *Monde*, the *Nouvel Observateur*, the *New York Times*, *France-Soir*, the *Guardian*, *Time*, *Newsweek*, *Esquire*, the *London Review of Books*, *Der Spiegel*, *Harper's*, the *Atlantic*, the *Boston Review* and so on. The printed page, Last had to admit, filled up a thin present where regret of the past and fear of the future had edged out any pleasure in looking at the moon or breathing the morning air or even fully absorbing the reams of print he read incessantly. He tried to imagine all that changing with Ariade. And now the possibility of quiet heroism. Meaning glimmered. Nor was it easy: he kept trying to look at the *Herald Tribune*. He finally scanned page one. After five o'clock, he went to a pay phone in the Metro and telephoned Howard. No news was good news and Last was to keep watching.

Last went into his hotel. As he ascended the stairs, Henri sang out that he had no mail. Last called Ariade. She invited him to her place, across the river in the Troisième, for a late supper.

Ariade had a sixth-floor flat. Everything was small: her bed, her teapot, her chairs, her bathroom, her television, the patch of flat roof onto which her single window opened. As she cooked, she told him about her wayward sister who lived in a stone shack, doing origami in the Pyrenees. Ariade had just turned thirty-six; she had hitchhiked from Buenos Aires to Chicago; in Texas, she had travelled briefly with a serial killer. She had book bags, handbags, earrings, necklaces and skirts made by Peruvian Indians. Yet she never looked like a rich liberal trying to pass as the wife of Atahualpa – she just looked like herself.

After supper, they sat sprawled on her bed looking at a 1920s atlas together. She sat or lay against him when it was easiest. They decided to go out for a late drink and she went into the bedroom to change. The door was open, the light was dim. Her shoulders and spine were smooth. From behind, he saw one of her breasts as it bobbed out. They went out to a local café. To Ariade's surprise, Last was able to keep up with her as they talked about late antiquity. She seemed intrigued by this man from nowhere: well-informed and with no known occupation. Last found her physically warm; intellectually tough. It was her touch that was extraordinary; she touched the back of his hand as she spoke, sometimes leaving her fingers there for a few seconds. At the Metro she kissed him twice on the mouth.

At the height of morning, on the terrace of the Metronome, he assessed every passerby near Chez Suzy. After a while, his gaze shifted to the upper stories over the restaurant. The sky was burnished by a dull sun. Ariade's body was probably full of surprises, her litheness concealing fullness, he thought, vaguely sensing the man in the photographs somewhere below, in his peripheral vision. There was only the slam of a car door. The car sped off out of sight. Last had a feeling it might have been an Audi. He felt a cold sweat; what a reason for twenty or thirty people to die.

The following day he watched Chez Suzy steadily; he thought he would go insane: the infinite tunnels of side streets and parked cars, the lines of balconies. At lunch, the terrace filled up. He watched every movement across the street: a chef having a smoke; two schoolgirls; a squat bowlegged man, perhaps a garage mechanic on his day off, bald, with a moustache and a leather jacket who turned to go into the *tabac* next to Chez Suzy and then reemerged. Last looked at his watch. The man approached, crossing the street, chewing a toothpick, opening a pack of cigarettes. He carried a package. He stepped up on the walk, edged between the tables. The only vacant seat was beside Last. The man sidled through and sat down. He placed the package on the table. It was addressed in Arabic. Last, terrified, picked up the *Guardian* and stared at the football score between Manchester and Tottenham. Hamadi smelt of lime aftershave; his breathing rattled. He ordered coffee, placed the toothpick in the ashtray, took out a cigarette.

"Vous avez du feu, s'il vous plaît?"

Last's forehead dampened. *"Oui."* He had matches for his single evening smoke. He lit Hamadi's cigarette, imagining it exploding and killing everyone. Hamadi inhaled, blew out the smoke, then wheezed. "English?" he said.

"Yeah." Hamadi's leather jacket was done right up; surely it was too warm. Maybe not. Maybe.

"I have known English from every English country," Hamadi said. On his fingers he listed: "English, Welsh, Scottish, Irish, American, Australian, New Zealand." He did a terrible imitation of an Irish, then a Scottish accent. Last forced a smile and a laugh.

"And you are from what?" Hamadi said.

"Canada."

"Yes!" Hamadi said, "I forget Canada!" Then he said, "Ow-ow-ow-o wow!" and laughed.

Last smiled. "Sorry?"

"You say 'ow'!" Hamadi said in English. "You say 'owww-t and abowwww-t.' Canadian!"

Last laughed. "We do say it that way."

Hamadi laughed. "You like Paris?" he said.

"It's all right." Last was trying to think of a way of leaving.

"You like the French people?" Hamadi said.

"Yeah. I don't mind them," Last said.

Hamadi said his girlfriend had been French. They had been talking about marriage but he had begun to suspect she was merely adventuring, using him to rebel against her family.

"She is always jealous of her older sister. Her older sister is in Borneo, secretly photographing the last cannibals as they are eating a German aid worker. So to compete with her, my girlfriend is going out with me. You imagine? An Arab in Paris. I am disgusted."

Last was staring at the package on the table. It seemed best to play along.

"Everything must have been even worse with 9/11," he said.

Hamadi looked at Last and extended his hand. Last shook it hesitantly.

"Yes. This is when it became worse." The girlfriend's mother was icily polite. Her father avoided meeting him. Her friends were full of phony smiles and fake liberal gestures. Four days ago, he and his girlfriend had broken up. No Arab man, let alone a Muslim could accept such a casual attitude toward love. Now his own friends had abandoned him as well. Hamadi cried quietly, tears running down his cheeks. He wiped his eyes. Last imagined his terrible isolation in Barbès Rochechouart, the big North African suburb, but couldn't think of anything to say.

"Well, time heals everything," he said blandly, nor did he believe it. Hamadi thought and nodded slowly. Last looked at his watch.

"I'd like to stay but I have to be somewhere," Last said and stood up. He extended his hand. Hamadi looked up at him.

"What is your name, Canadian friend?"

"Phil." The name came to mind.

Hamadi squeezed his hand and said, "Phil, I am Ali. You have say more to me in these twenty minutes than anyone say in a whole year. Especially what you say about time. About time, I have read St. Augustine. In Arabic translation. If you are here again, I see you here."

Last used the pay phone at his own Metro stop, St. Michel. On the other end, Howard was silent.

"Where'd he go?" he finally said.

"I don't know. I left."

"You should have stayed."

Now Last was silent.

"I'm sorry," Howard continued, "but you gotta stay on him. I didn't realize you'd speak to him. It's just we got a crisis... All right, here's what we're going to do. I'm gonna warn Defense to change the restaurant again. I want you to go back; if he's there, chat with him, pick up anything he says. If it's easy to tail him, tail him. Don't take any risks."

That evening, Last met Ariade at an exhibit of photographs by a British traveller in Siberia in 1904. *"C'est tout à fait Rocambolesque,"* she said. Then they went up to her place for supper. The occasion was a TV interview with Bernard-Henri Lévy, surely a pretext. It seemed the moment had come.

They watched the program sitting on a covered day bed. As it concluded, she leaned heavily on his thigh; as she reached for some matches, her breast, in light cotton, brushed his face. Last moved to kiss her, his mouth just missing hers as she glided back with the matches. Indicating Lévy's smiling, white-shirted image as it faded on the TV, he kidded her saying, *"C'est tout à fait Potemkinesque."* He leaned toward her again but she stood up, hotly defending Lévy. Then she got ready for bed; the bathroom door was open a half inch. Her nakedness flickered back and forth. She came out in a dressing gown. *"Alors,"* she said, clapping briskly. It was time to go. She saw Last to the door. She kissed him three times on the mouth. She said, *"À la prochaine."* Last went out into the brutality of the night.

The following day was Saturday and the terrace of the Metronome was packed. Last went down to the washroom and when he came back, Hamadi was sitting toward the end of the terrace. He was writing something. Last decided to stay inside the restaurant, back from the glass doors. It became clear that Hamadi was sketching. He was looking at Chez Suzy. Hamadi pushed the paper inside his jacket and left.

Last lost him twice, picked him up twice, followed him to a Metro station. The platform was crowded. Last caught the car behind the one Hamadi took and watched him through the interconnecting doors. At Barbès Rochechouart he tailed him out into the packed streets filled with men in gellabas, prayer caps, veiled women, cars, cafés and motor scooters. In a big old café, he saw Hamadi talk to the Arab proprietor for a long time. Then Hamadi went into a dark shawarma place. Last pretended to look through the cheap saris of a Bengalese merchant as he glanced through the dark door of the fast-food shop. Hamadi was playing pinball. It went on for two hours. It began to rain. As the saris started to get wet, the Bengali began to close down the display racks. Last was out in the open. In the downpour, he watched from a doorway. Hamadi took out a cigarette, lit it and played more. Time passed. He came out into the rain. He walked toward Last. Last turned and pushed his face into painted Arabic lettering on a window. He sensed Hamadi moving on. He waited and followed.

In a side street, in the downpour, Hamadi disappeared. Last took the Metro and went to the Bar Mazet near his hotel where he telephoned Howard. Howard seemed tense, probably because Last had stumbled into something beyond his competence. Quietly and distinctly Howard said that, according to their information, any attempt at a bombing would be carried out by Hamadi.

"Howard," Last said, "this isn't my area of judgement. But I honestly don't think a man who could be devastated by a woman could kill a lot of innocent strangers."

Howard said he would recommend they change the restaurant again and asked Last to continue watching for Hamadi.

It was just past four. Last called Ariade and she invited him up. When he got there, she was in a bikini, shining with suntan lotion, bubbled with sweat. She asked that he take off his shoes because of the roof. He sat on a towel barefoot and in his shirtsleeves. She lay on a towel, on her stomach. He told her about Howard and his boredom as head of the economic section; his jogging, his guilelessness. As she laughed she sat up and reached behind, pulling the string of her top. Last stared into the distance, describing Howard's Louis XV salon with the PlayStation and the trophies. She shook with laughter. He thought she would hold her top to her chest and lie face down again but she sat up, her breasts, slightly paler than the rest of her, bobbing down, and coming to rest. He talked about liking Howard, how rare it was now that he met anyone he liked.

"Really, why?" she said. He thought she was going to replace her top but instead she spread lotion on her arms.

"I don't know," he said. "People aren't reflective. Even when they have money, they're preoccupied with practical matters, real estate, bargains, survival. Prices, opportunities. As if there were nothing else."

"That's so true," she said. "You have wisdom, did you know that?"

He knew it wasn't true. She lay on her back, her breasts settling. He glanced to his left and saw the cupola of Les Invalides in the haze, then looked down at his feet. Her nipples were a light pink. He let some silence pass and asked her, "What do you think of when you're alone?"

"My parents in the Ardèche, my sister, old lovers. My doctorate." She paused and said, "I think of you."

He looked off into the heat haze.

"I think of you too," he said.

"What do you think of?" she said.

He couldn't think. "Your sandals," he said.

"My sandals?"

He was stuck. It had something to do with her hair and her eyes and the way she thought. The feeling he had was senseless, exalted, useless. It must be love. It made him happy.

Last spent all of the next day at the Metronome watching Chez Suzy but Hamadi didn't appear. Perhaps they knew of Defense's change of location.

The following day he went back up to Barbès. The huge old corner café where Hamadi had talked to the proprietor was a busy hybrid place that sold *café au lait* and hot lamb. More confident now, Last had come with the *Sydney Review of Books*, the *New York Review of Books*, the *New York Times*, the *London Review of Books*, the *Nouvel Observateur* and the *Sunday Times*. This time he wore sunglasses. He spent all day there without seeing Hamadi. He spent all of the next day without seeing Hamadi either, watching the crowds as he glanced about between movie reviews, reviews of a new biography of George Eliot, a piece on the culture wars at Duke University and so on. On Tuesday he had shawarma with Arabic tea and read a piece about the end of Toronto's urban dream in the English *Der Speigel*. He read the *Monde*. There was no sign of Hamadi. Last even returned and watched Chez Suzy briefly. Back in Barbes he sat in the huge crowded café all day Wednesday and Thursday. On Friday he was coming back out to the terrace with lamb on a baguette when he stopped dead. Hamadi was walking across the intersection.

Four streets away, Hamadi disappeared into a doorway. Last made a note of the address. In fifteen minutes a black Mercedes pulled up. A thin, hatchet-faced man got out. Hamadi came back out of the doorway, wearing a sweat suit, and he and the tall man got into the car. Last wrote down the plate number.

He took the Metro down to the Bar Mazet and called Howard. There was no answer. He phoned Ariade. There was no answer there either. At the hotel, Henri gave him a note that said: *Luxembourg, 6 pm.* He imagined Ariade, or perhaps an exotic Moroccan woman dropping off the enigmatic note. Henri smiled and said, "A little American boy with a toy catamaran left it."

There was time to kill. Ariade had finished a seminar at the Sorbonne and they met for a coffee. Last told her that he had thought of moving to Italy.

"To write poetry?"

"No."

"What would you do there?"

"Maybe teach English, maybe nothing at all," Last said. "Walk a lot. Use it as a place to travel from."

"A lot of people I know have become very critical of Italy," she said.

"Who is it that doesn't like Italy?" Last asked.

She paused and said, "Jean-Luc."

"Who's Jean-Luc?"

"My husband."

"Your husband?"

"He's coming back in October. We live together and apart. He's got a job in Italy. It's better for us that way."

"You never mentioned your husband."

"Should I have?"

Last said nothing. She looked at him, shading her eyes in the strong low sun, making a perplexed laugh. They went to the Metro.

She kissed him as they parted.

At six, Last sat in the Luxembourg Gardens watching the little sailboats pushed across the pond by children. He wondered what Ariade was doing with him, whether or not she would sleep with him, if she really loved Jean-Luc. He imagined himself making her happy into old age, then imagined it all ending, or what little there was, ending tomorrow. He read *Time* magazine. After an interval, he heard a terrible buzzing sound. Among the toy boats was a large, plastic, radio-controlled catamaran. It bullied about, pushing the sailboats out of the way. He could not see the boy. With the deafening sound of a metal chair on gravel, Howard sat down beside Last, holding a remote control.

"Thank God you're here." He directed the toy catamaran. The little boy, his son, came up beside him and tried to take it. Howard pulled it away, evaded him.

"Why?" said Last.

"There's a lot of chatter."

"How do you mean chatter?"

"I couldn't talk to you on the line. A lot of Internet and cell phone chatter. Something's being planned. I hope they're not onto us. We moved the dinner again. We're having our phone security, all our encryption checked."

The little boy came up and said something about his sister. Howard started to say "Fuck" but stood up, passing the remote control to his son.

Howard and Last went into the trees where a French girl about eleven tended the two-year-old girl in a stroller.

"It's the *au pair*'s day off," Howard said. "Cathy's horseback riding."

"Right."

"So what did you see?" Howard said, laying a blanket on the stone table and hoisting the child up with a change bag. Last told him about Hamadi in Barbès, the street address, the hatchet-faced man and the Mercedes. Howard began to change the child. Last gave him a paper with the address and the licence number. Howard cleaned the little girl with wipes. This was probably something Last would never know; long ago, he and his wife had conceived twins but they had died in childbirth.

"My uninformed...sense," Last said, "is that the real problem is the guy with the Mercedes."

"Well, we know otherwise." Howard balled up the used diaper and tied it in a plastic bag. "It's Hamadi. Anyway, you're done. I thank you for this. We'll take it from here. You cannot tell anyone about this, anyone at all. The French would lodge a protest and the State Department would use it in their feud with us and with Defense and on and on."

"It never happened," Last said.

"Exactly."

They walked to the pond. Howard jabbed a finger at him: "We'll have a drink. Soon." Directing the remote control and sending the catamaran zooming at high speed around a sail-boat, Howard extended his hand.

"Absolutely," Last said. They shook hands.

On Tuesday, Last was on his way out through the hotel lobby when he caught the word "suicide" on the radio. He stopped but the newscast was ending. Henri smiled at Last and gently explained, as if to a child, that an unidentified man, believed to be Muslim, was just trying to blow up a restaurant near Bastille but was shot before entering, upon which his explosives detonated. Henri's opinion was that it was the work of an obscure Saudi Arabian sect of Salafis angered by the import of French digital film technology. He drew parallels with a group of dissident 12th-century Ismailis. Last wasn't listening. He waved to Henri, went to the Bar Mazet, and telephoned Howard.

"It was the guy," Howard said.

"Which guy?"

But Howard just said, "Seven pm," gave an address and hung up.

In a street in the Septième, Last was let in through a door in a wall by an old woman who led him through some alleys into the courtyard where they had had the barbecue. In the salon, places for a late, informal supper were set. As they ate, Cathy smiled sadly at Last.

After dinner, Last and Howard sat in the armchairs. Cathy played solitaire on a laptop and the six-year-old watched a tape of *How the Grinch Stole Christmas* behind them. Howard lit a cigar. "Defense set up the dinner at the last minute in Le Périgord, a place in Bastille. The man with the Mercedes was Asadi Ben Rumi. I had Hamadi tailed and I had Ben Rumi tailed just to make sure. But our focus was on Hamadi – we followed him to the Boulevard des Italiens to see if he was heading for Bastille. Meanwhile, guess who shows up at Le Périgord? Your driver, there, of the Mercedes. Ben Rumi. But he doesn't have the Mercedes. He's heading for the door, dressed like a businessman who could be walking into that lunch. Hamadi apparently was a diversion; Ben Rumi was the real thing. Security got him. He detonated in the street. Two passersby were injured. Nobody in the restaurant was harmed. A lot of broken windows."

Last contemplated his role in the man's death. Howard was staring at him. "You saved twenty lives. Possibly more," he said. Last looked at the floor.

Howard explained that Last was not to take it personally but he was now an "infected asset": he had spoken with the man he was to watch. He was in no great danger but ought to be a little vigilant anywhere he was in Paris.

Cathy sat down and they had drinks. The conversation veered perilously close to Last's degree of success as a poet; he steered it deftly away but it came back again. Again he deflected it but the absence of a reputation more or less asserted itself. The Juarezes didn't seem to care. They all had a final nightcap. Howard looked at the floor. "I don't know what to say," he said. "I'm sending you a thousand bucks. It's off the books. You saved a lot of lives. I mean, they would have been lost. I can shoot you twenty thousand. From a contingency fund. It wouldn't be missed. Money's wasted all the time anyway. It'd probably go to something less worthwhile."

Last didn't want the twenty thousand but didn't feel he could say why. Howard responded to Last's silence.

"You don't have to declare it," Howard said.

"I realize that."

They walked Last to the front door.

"You ever been to Syria?" Howard asked.

"No. Why?"

"Would you be interested?"

An image materialized of cafés in Damascus – the *New York Review of Books*, the *Herald Tribune*, *Books in Canada* ...a hotel with someone irritating on the desk. The endless walking, the coffees day by day, the depression, the boredom.

"Let's talk about it," Last said.

On Sunday Ariade was sunbathing on the roof. This time Last sat on a chair, his bare feet on the tin. She sat, her back propped against the wall, her eyes closed. Her breasts were covered with lotion.

"That's the way it is," she said. "I'm attracted to you, but it's not love. I like touching you. I'm a very tactile person. I feel sensual when I'm with you."

Last contemplated the humid sky.

"But it's not sex," she said. "At least not sex in the usual sense. Which I think is what you mean. I'm more interested in companionship than in involvement. A companionship with sensuality." She went on to imply that his interpretation of her physicality was somehow adolescent. There was no point in saying anything. Against his better judgement, he uttered a few disjointed phrases. It served only to bring her to the point.

"You don't have a feeling of freedom about you. I need that sense of freedom – that existential sense, where your identity is something you throw off when you look into the abyss." She paused. "Jean-Luc and I are going bungee jumping in the Loire."

Last wondered what had happened to the château district. He let the sweat run into his eyes. A panorama stretched from the corner of his eye: the dome of Les Invalides and the shimmering spire of St. Germain, the edge of the roof, the wall in sunlight, her breasts as finely wrought and indifferent as the city itself. He felt a tremendous damming up of time; he too was borne on the flood, the swelling debris of thoughts, waste, splendor, dead ideologies, broken Corinthian columns, pornography, silverware, computers, used condoms, candy wrappers, forgotten conversations, wrecked trucks. Somewhere in the tide, twenty or thirty people in a restaurant had been saved. There, at least, was something good. For himself, nothing would change. He left Ariade's for the last time.

Perhaps he would see Howard and Cathy again. The head of the CIA station in Paris and his wife were lonely. The twenty thousand dollars he would not accept. The seventy dollars per day that it cost him to live, on savings, had already set a limit to his life; a limit he preferred. Hamadi may have seen him again; a Muslim radical group may suspect him by now but he found he didn't care. What would come would come. As to Howard's proposal of the job in Syria, he would flip a coin.

Without knowing why, he went into the church of Les Invalides. The four hundred rotting battle flags were still ranged in dusty grandeur, like garments of the dead, the gold inscriptions august and numinous, as they had been on the day they had been handed to the regiments two hundred years before. And, suddenly, like so much else, more tremendous for their utter irrelevance. Last found himself weeping and went out. Along the Seine the haze had turned to a silent storm; the light faded. It was as if he were disappearing into a painted landscape; into a bounded world of gentle meaning; and in it still, and until dark at least, the sense of something ecstatic and impending.

THE MAN

The girls said it was the man. A car accident up the street; chrome and blue sky and a crowd. They said you could see red. The older sister, Karen, went up ahead and the younger one, Wendy, said, "There's blood!" She grabbed my arm and pulled me up the walk. I was only four then and wanted to go but yet I was afraid. I tried to see the red under the crowd and the murmur of police radios and the girls kept moving ahead and I was afraid and kept pulling back.

"It's the man!" Karen said.

The girls were five and seven and had a smell of oldness, of having lived: their grey skin, their faded, greyish dresses, their stained teeth, the thick wildness of their hair. They were saying that maybe the man had caused the accident and then I thought the man was lying under the car. They let go and ran on and I followed them, but slowly, because I was afraid that if I went there they'd take me further into the hot haze and blood and falling darkness and I would be gone forever. Finally I turned and went back down the street to my house.

There were railway tracks up past the street in the distance, and in the weeks that followed I'd hear the trains pass and I'd lie awake, thinking of the accident and the man.

The next time I heard of the man, the girls had taken me all the way up to where the accident had been. They turned and took me along the main street to a corner store and I was afraid of the sun going down. They suddenly became mothers taking me shopping and there was a man called the manager in a white apron staring at them and Karen said, "Hurry, they're closing!" It was because the manager in the apron knew the man and if we were late he would send the man after us. I wanted to go home but Karen had a basket on her arm, her hands hanging with busy self-importance, and she told Wendy to load the basket. The man in the apron watched while the girls counted coins and then he told them to put everything back and they rushed to put it all back, looking for whatever they could pay for. The lights flashed and the man shouted, "Make it snappy," and the lights were going off one by one and we ran out and I thought the man was coming after us and the girls were screaming and pulling me because I couldn't run as fast.

When we were walking and I was out of breath, Wendy pulled five barrettes and three packs of gum from her dress and Karen said, "You shouldn't of. You're going to get it," and Wendy said, "So? They're not going to know."

"The man will find out," Karen said.

"No, he won't," Wendy said. "The man wasn't there."

"The man's gonna kill us. He knows where we live. He knows where Henry lives."

I thought the man would come to get me and I started to cry. The setting sun shone low along the street where the accident had been.

"He doesn't know we were there," Wendy said.

"He lives across the street. He's going to see us," Karen said. "He's a murderer. He killed someone. There was so much blood, it filled up the basement."

I went into my house and my mother said good night to the girls on the porch. As she put me to bed, I tried to tell her about the man but she said it was all right. When I began to sleep there came the sound of the train that ran along in the distance beside Dupont Street, where the accident had been, in a clacking whisper-roar, a sleeping rush that came as the man suddenly stood up in a brown suit by a wash basin in an attic room lit by a setting sun, red as blood, and there was blood in the basin.

That summer, I played in the moss and clinker and scattered coal by the basement windows of the big old houses; I played under dark sash windows speckled with rain dust, windows that shook when trucks passed and reflected cars at night. Somewhere, as evening came, the man was always in an upper room, under a sloping ceiling, just like my own room, and Wendy said that he slept all day and wakened at sunset, and only then did he wash the blood from his hands.

Wendy and Karen and I and an older girl with glasses called Judy and a sleepy kid called Arthur were on my front lawn and we fell on top of each other, laughing, in a game of Ring Around the Rosie when someone said something about having to be home at dark, but then they were on the sidewalk and I went with them around the block to a street I had seen once before and Karen was saying, "He's too little," and though the sun was going down, I didn't want to be too little, so I went with them.

They went far and now I was more afraid to go back alone than to go on with them. The street lights were coming on and they were starting to run ahead of me and I was trying to keep up and not be afraid.

We got to a big street and there were no houses on the other side, just the last of the sky and a twinkling star, and Karen broke into a run, long-legged like a boy, and her legs, then her waist disappeared downward in the dark as if she were being eaten from below by darkness. But it was a hill going down and Karen was ahead and someone said, "Christie Pits." They were gone in windy open darkness and there was a loud bang and sparks. I turned to run and I was jerked back by my arm and Wendy and the others were running, wild, in blowing wind in the dark and there were voices of boys or men and a man in a white shirt and smoke drifting and Karen was there and then was swallowed up and someone yelled, "The man!" and there was hysterical screaming.

Wendy came out of the dark so that I wasn't lost and she said, "Come on!" Karen was screaming to Wendy, "Don't show him! Let's get out of here." They passed a street lamp and a spattering of blood on pavement, red where it pooled, black where it was thin. We were near the edge of the park where the hill went up and Wendy said, "Stay there. Don't move," and pulled down her underpants and peed and stood up flicking up her dress and I saw her vagina, a naked "V" in the pale light as she pulled up her underpants, and Karen yelled at her from a distance, "You stole. I told you." Then they were running up the hill now and my chest was hurting and the man was coming after us to kill us, and I knew I would die because I was behind and couldn't run fast enough.

Wendy ran back and got me and in a while we came to our street. My chest was hurting and my face was wet and I ran in the front door and my mother whacked me on the behind.

Every day I wondered if the man was coming, because Wendy had stolen. Sometimes the man was in the upper room. Sometimes he came down the street, covered with blood from the accident. The man, in his brown suit, could come sound-lessly into your house at night and kill you in your sleep. The man was in the western sky. At night, in the dark, I could feel his hands on my neck.

In the fall, when Wendy and Karen were in school, I watched television. I watched *Popeye* and black-and-white seas and an eastern land with minarets and domes and a sky that was grey like the sky outside the window, the sky under which the man slept.

~ ~ ~

After I started school, my mother took me a few doors up and in through a driveway between two immense walls of houses and into a paved yard where a great elm thrust the concrete into shards, and by the back door there was a thin blond boy, younger than I was, playing with a truck under a forsythia bush. My mother introduced him as Stephen and said to stay there until she came back. Stephen looked up at me, frowning, and recited his address, the city, the province, the country.

I asked Stephen if he knew about the man.

"His name is Mr. Gimble," Stephen said.

I extended the road in the dirt for Stephen's truck and said, "The man is a murderer. He murders people."

Stephen stood up and looked to the west, closed one eye in concentration and extended a crooked finger, saying, "He comes from over that way."

"The girls across the street said he's coming."

"My parents said not to talk about him," Stephen said. "He used to live here."

"He used to live in your house?"

"I'm not sure. He might live next door."

Stephen's family lived on the top two floors and on the second floor, in the dining room, you could see across the drive and through the neighbours' half-drawn blinds and curtains into big dark rooms where dim figures did things without sound. In Stephen's living room, another window looked sideways to a two-storey veranda and above it you could see the dormer where the girls might have said the man lived. Stephen was pretty sure it was Mr. Gimble. The house was full of a big Ukrainian family, the Dirvitches – the father, the mother, the children, aunts, uncles, a grandmother and a couple of roomers. My parents had said that roomers were a bad influence and Stephen speculated that they might be murderers. As Stephen's mother was giving us lunch, Stephen said that Mr. Gimble had sneaked downstairs in the night and carried away Luba Dirvitch's little sister and suffocated her.

"Don't be silly," Stephen's mother said. "Mr. Gimble is running for alderman and he has personal problems and anything you overhear you must not repeat." Whatever that meant, it was only another indication that Mr. Gimble was a danger.

Stephen and I would discuss the problem of Mr. Gimble as we played in my yard or around Stephen's garage. We'd talk about how tall Mr. Gimble was and how quickly he could come. In the corner of my yard, with water from a hose, we dug a hole which would tunnel under continents, eventually trapping Mr. Gimble, and then chase him up through the earth to China which was also west, over the sky, beyond the other side of the block. In the basement of Stephen's house, Stephen turned on his grandfather's radio with its short-wave band and we listened to a shaking carnival sound through static and Stephen said the music came from the land of Mr. Gimble. We fitted some old plumbing through a fruit crate with a funnel for a mouth and an elbow joint for a penis and decided it was Mr. Gimble and poured water through it so that it urinated. This was the potion we kept giving to Mr. Gimble to put him to sleep so we could escape from the basement.

Stephen was always reflecting, calculating. He already knew about numbers. Though he wasn't yet in school, his mother was teaching him to add three and two in pencil on the surface of the enamel table in their kitchen. I didn't see the point of adding three and two.

One Saturday, Stephen and I met Karen and Wendy on the sidewalk and I said, "They know about Mr. Gimble."

"My mother said he's the murderer," Stephen said.

Karen looked at Wendy and said, "Should we tell them?"

"Tell them what?" Karen said.

"That he's the man. All the blood. Over on Euclid Avenue."

Stephen visored his eyes with his hand and frowned at the girls in the sunlight.

"Who's the little guy?" Karen said.

"Stephen."

"Why's he so small?" Wendy said.

"He's my friend," I said.

On the third floor of Stephen's house, on the carpet in his father's study, Stephen and I did a jigsaw puzzle of Zorro in Mexico. I said even Zorro had never found Mr. Gimble and Stephen said that Mr. Gimble had gone through Mexico. I said that the girls had seen Mr. Gimble but Stephen said they were trying to fool me.

~ ~ ~

Winter came and the girls were gone. They didn't leave, they didn't even move away. They were simply gone. I had never even known where they lived, only that they lived across the street. I remembered their hair, their dresses, their mysterious violence and their stories and secrecy and the infinite profane wonder that lay far back, behind Wendy's grey skin and freckles.

Children whose names I knew, like Arthur and Judy, were gone and so were all the others. My parents said they had moved somewhere called the suburbs.

Stephen and I began to watch television at each other's houses and then one Sunday I was in our third-floor spare room and through the window onto the alley I saw into the neighbour's window: a room as dark as a fish tank with a strip of burning sunlight on the wall as if a shadow could enter and cross it. I telephoned Stephen and said that Mr. Gimble had moved next door.

Mr. Gimble still wakened and washed his hands and Stephen said that it was time to figure out where he travelled from and returned to. We went outside and copied street signs onto a map. As rain fell in the alley outside the study in my house, we expanded the map to Bathurst and Huron, Bloor to Dupont where the accident had been. The map ended with the train tracks and the escarpment. We marked points on the periphery where Mr. Gimble had been sighted. We added the railway tracks and the Midtown Cinema.

That November, Stephen and I redrew the map, including an enlarged detail with a plan of Stephen's driveway and the garage and the Dirvitch house, and when we were out there checking the map, Luba Dirvitch, who was younger, asked what we were doing. We showed her and she said it wasn't allowed and went in and told her mother. Mrs. Dirvitch came outside and Stephen nervously said we were only waiting until his mother came back to give us lunch. Mrs. Dirvitch asked us if we wanted some soup.

The Dirvitches' kitchen was full of steam and the smell of cabbage and as we ate, and Luba watched us suspiciously, we kept glancing down the hall into the darkness which seemed to go on forever and tried to stop laughing about Mr. Gimble. From the Dirvitches' kitchen, Stephen's house, the driveway and the garage and the tree that broke through the concrete looked familiar but unfamiliar: Stephen's house from the other side, skewed and through steam, as if from a different world.

~ ~ ~

In September, Stephen was sent to a local grade school and I was sent to a Catholic school that was well to the north, beyond the escarpment, beyond the boundary of the map. On the first day at my school, a lot of the kids in class were talking and the old woman teacher threatened everyone with the strap, and told us if we weren't sorry in our heart we would go to hell and we'd burn. If we'd ever been burned by a cigarette, it would be like that but all over our body and forever.

School loomed above the escarpment, a world of older boys with pointed shoes who smoked cigarettes and greeted each other with a kick to the groin, or Italian girls who already had earrings and breasts, of kids who would knock your hat off to make you hit back so they could beat you up, of teachers who yelled and screamed or made you stand up and ridiculed you. I didn't do as well in school as Stephen did.

When my father was travelling and after the housekeeper left at noon, my mother would sleep for long periods. Sometimes in the evening, when she gave me my dinner, her eyelids would be heavy and she'd tell me I didn't love her. When my father returned, I overheard him arguing with my mother about her drinking.

Sometimes at dinner, when my father was away, my mother would sit staring at me, periodically losing consciousness. There would be no lights on and the sun would be setting and her eyes would open and she'd pick up where she'd left off, telling me that she knew what was going on in my soul and that I hated her, that they were worried about me and were thinking of sending me away. Then she would slump over sideways.

At school, I didn't make friends and always looked forward to getting home, but once home I'd look forward to getting to Stephen's up the street. When I'd mention to Stephen what I'd learned about God and hell, Stephen would have no comment. Stephen seemed to live in a house that was simple and austere in pale light, like the Dutch picture in his living room of a woman in the grey light of a window, the picture itself in the pale light of the window of Stephen's living room.

Stephen's mother had decided he should attend the local Anglican church service and I noticed the jacket and new, awkward-looking brown shoes that Stephen's mother had bought him for Sundays. But in a while it became clear that for Stephen's family, church didn't really matter. In the end, Stephen only went once.

One day, when my mother had passed out and gone to bed, I had dinner at Stephen's and Stephen said that his parents had been talking about moving to Montreal. As I went home that night, the street lights came on and I wondered what would happen when Stephen was gone.

That spring, I was still hoping the move to Montreal would be forgotten when we started writing a play about Mr. Gimble. Mr. Gimble was always somewhere offstage and the characters, a lion, a bear and an elephant, wondered what to do on his approach and the animals had arguments about how to deal with him. The play was called "The Man." In the end, the animals were pursued by Mr. Gimble through mountain and forest and finally caves until the lion and the elephant escaped by deserting the bear. Mr. Gimble tried to kill the bear, but he sank in quicksand and the bear escaped. We didn't find happy endings interesting and we had the bear wander off, wounded and bloody, looking forever for the lion and the elephant.

Stephen was now taller than I was, and thin. Stephen was seven and I was eight but Stephen could already calculate the difference between our weights, multiply it by itself, subtract the weight difference from the product and that would be the height of Mr. Gimble. On weekends now, we wrote a newspaper named for the block. It had its stock page, its news, its women's and sports sections, much of the paper related to Mr. Gimble, all written in columns on lined, legal-sized paper.

Stephen decided that according to the map of the world, Mr. Gimble lived in Rio de Janeiro. I was skeptical and to settle it, we played Pirate and Traveler in Stephen's basement and if either of us landed on Rio de Janeiro, it meant Mr. Gimble was there. I landed on Rio de Janeiro and we argued until we found a compromise. Mr. Gimble was in several places at once. What was more, Mrs. Dirvitch and Mr. Gimble had been lovers and Mrs. Dirvitch had betrayed Mr. Gimble by evicting him and now lived in fear. There was no longer any doubt about Mr. Gimble's other residence when, one Saturday in his basement, Stephen turned the dial of his grandfather's radio and through static on the short-wave band were voices, remote and elegiac, with shaking music. Near the red line on the yellow dial was "Rio de Janeiro."

By Christmas, the bear had staggered, wounded, to Toronto, and Mrs. Dirvitch knew it was only a matter of time before Mr. Gimble would be resurrected from the quicksand outside Rio de Janeiro. The ever-nearing presence had now taken on some urgency and Stephen believed the man, Mr.

Gimble, could in theory be located using the stars and he got an astronomy book. Finally, on a map, we drew in the heavens according to the points on the compass. Stephen went into his backyard and squinted at the night sky, again with one eye closed, the same way he had squinted at me when we had first met under the forsythia, the pencil now waving in his thin hand as he slowly marked and erased.

Another year and Stephen's family still hadn't moved. After school now, as the street lights blinked on, Stephen and I played ball hockey with boys from Stephen's school on the broken concrete drive. Sometimes, just the two of us played, opening the garage and improvising goal posts against the back wall, and the opposing goal where the houses narrowed the driveway. When there were enough to make teams, we played fast and violently around the big elm and through crumbled leaves, slapping the ball out of the Dirvitches' wild roses until suppertime when the backs of houses became shadows and the cold was intoxicating, and in the last of the freezing red azure the world was still alive and violent.

~ ~ ~

When the snow had gone and the streets were dirty and damp, Stephen and I went west as far as we could go, into the land where Mr. Gimble had walked. The houses were a little smaller and a lot of the people spoke Italian or other languages and there were more corner stores. It was getting time to turn back when a girl around our age, who was neither white nor black, perhaps a dark Italian or something else, smiled at us, chewing gum, and asked us, grinning, if we wanted to play games in her basement. We were courteous and asked her what the games were.

"Wait and see," she said, laughing.

We discussed it and Stephen looked at his watch and decided it would be better to get back.

"You don't know what you're missin'," she said. "Prizes and then surprises!" and she laughed.

That spring, after his ninth birthday, Stephen spoke importantly of what he called "my condition," something he called his lymph. I would ask him about it but Stephen wouldn't say much more. Soon Stephen was in bed. In July, Stephen's mother and sister got mad at me and told me not to bother Stephen; he had to rest. In August, I didn't see Stephen at all.

My parents and I brought Stephen puzzles and books in the hospital and I brought the latest edition of the newspaper and its reports on Mr. Gimble, but without Stephen's calculations and geography. On Thanksgiving, at the hospital, Stephen was an odd colour and hardly spoke. In December my parents and I went down to an Anglican funeral home. I was told to stay with my aunt out in the lobby, but through the doors I glimpsed the awkward brown shoes at the end of the coffin; the shoes Stephen had worn only once.

On a clear night in January, I went outside his house and saw the overturned bowl of the firmament, the stars and planets that had their centre above the block, with a planet over Bathurst Street and a constellation over Spadina Road and the shifting skies that tracked the man, ever shifting, but now more distant.

I tried to do another copy of the newspaper but it was difficult. I tried again but I couldn't and I left it. By the study window there was the light of a grey day in the alley, grey like the day we started the play about Mr. Gimble. But I watched television now. I watched it all the time. Sometimes the black-and-white seas in *Popeye* brought the old skies back, the skies of Rio de Janeiro.

One Wednesday I came home from school very tired and barely finished my homework. The following morning I wakened with my throat sore and my head congested and my mother kept me at home. I had trouble sleeping at night for the heat in my face, and difficulty breathing. In my dreams, the corners of the room would fade into sparkling darkness and the floor would give way into nothing. In the day, I lay in bed and watched television until I had too much trouble breathing. I spent two days in hospital and then my father took me home and now I slept heavily.

I wakened on a Friday, still in the study, and it was raining in the alley and my mother told me they had brought my fever down. Apparently I had nearly died. I got up and moved to the window and saw a glimmer of moss among cracked bricks and the alley was alive with rain. She told me it was April. I dressed and went outside.

The outlines were there, what you saw was there, but everything else was gone. I remembered the two sisters, Wendy and Karen, and things came back with the sound of the train that still passed by at the end of the street. I remembered Arthur and Judy and faces that had never had names.

I went down Stephen's driveway, past the elm, the broken concrete. By the back door and the forsythia I found Stephen's hockey stick and took shots against the back wall of the garage and Mrs. Dirvitch returned from shopping and asked me if I wanted soup. In the kitchen there was the steam and the cabbage smell, and then outside, the strangeness of Stephen's house, still there but the other way, distant and backwards. I asked to use the bathroom and Mrs. Dirvitch told me it was upstairs and I went up. I stopped at the door to a big shabby bedroom and saw that it was the mirror image of Stephen's dining room, through the windows. I went in and looked across the alley to Stephen's dining room and like a dream saw myself and Stephen at the table, writing the newspaper.

After I was back at school, I tried to stay away from my parents by watching television or staying in my room or by walking the surrounding streets. One day I went farther west, as if I were going off the edge of the earth, all the way west to where Mr. Gimble had been.

These streets had endless pillared porches under a different sky. Someone said "Hi" and I turned and saw the grinning dark girl and she said, "Do you remember me?" She asked me if I wanted some pop and I said okay. She took me down an alley and into a basement rec room and gave me a sickly-sweet cherry soda then turned on a television and introduced me to *American Bandstand.* I mimicked the singers and she doubled up laughing. We had a pushing contest on the sofa and our laughter was drowned by the roar of the train and Mr. Gimble was in the distance and the train receded and she said, teasing, "Will you go steady with me?" A woman yelled from upstairs and footsteps were coming down and the girl told me I had to get out fast and she held out her arms operatically but I just laughed and ran out. I set off for home thinking of her and then turned and tried to remember where her house was. I looked up: Stephen would have said something about it being under Orion, Orion the hunter.

One evening in September, when I'd started Grade II, my father and mother remarked that Alderman Gimble had gone on trial for using municipal funds to entertain his mistress. Later, I saw him on the news on television: weedy and balding with a pencil moustache and horn-rimmed glasses, waving away reporters.

On a night at home, my mother and father were having coffee and my mother said the bank robber, Bill Gimley, had died in prison. He'd been famed for his sharp brown suits and he'd been living in a rooming house near Christie Pits when it was believed, though never proven, that he'd murdered a suspected informer who was found with his throat cut on the third floor, and in another room there was a basin filled with bloody water. Later, I learned that Wendy and Karen had lived in a basement across the street and that their mother had been a prostitute.

In Grade II, I liked to pretend I was from nowhere and dress in an anonymous trench coat. After school, I'd get off the bus at a diner, a few blocks from home, and sit and do my homework and read the newspaper while the trains passed, shaking the cereal boxes and rattling the cups. One day in April, I'd just left the diner when I saw the girl coming towards me over the water from the melting snow that ran across the walks. She had a body now and wore a ski jacket. She lived in the same house but this time we went up to the third floor and sat cross-legged on the bed in her room. It was the same game of laughing but soon we were tangled together, half-naked, and there was a noise downstairs and she jumped out of bed, wearing only a sleeveless undershirt, and below it the unexpected luxuriance of pubic hair in a band of late sunlight and the train passed, roaring.

It was a long train and I could hear it still going away as I left and I realized I was walking away from home. Dark fell fast and I was in Christie Pits and the wind was wild, the light standards swaying, the pools of light moving in cold abandonment, the wind roaring in the trees and I thought, It's still there, it's all still there, we've been taught in school about things ending and new things beginning. But none of it's true, it's all wrong, it doesn't end. Because I was looking up and Stephen was there among the stars, in the firmament, the whole thing alive and numinous, and the great shadow even yet stalking among the houses of the west. And I thought, I know I'll be with that girl again, but I also know Wendy and Karen are there too, and even if they're dead they're alive and the fact is, you carry it with you, all of it, as sure as the hunter is fixed, emblazoned in the night sky, as sure as his name is Orion.

THROUGH THE SKY

He raced ahead on his tricycle, up the walk, past all the blue sky in chrome fenders, past the milk horse and wagon, the sidewalk reared up and the man was there, the man who had lived upstairs, standing in front of a house a few doors up, the heavy trees, the hot sun and shadow on asphalt, talking to the girls from across the street. The boy stopped his tricycle, the girls screaming, and Wendy said, "He's going to show us the castle, you can see through the trees and the castle all the way to the sky." The man was in a sleeveless undershirt, smoking a cigarette, hair greased back, sandals and socks and the glint of a gold tooth.

"Where?" the boy, Henry, said.

"Up there," she pointed. "Upstairs, at his place. And he says if we can guess the name of the story, he's going to show us a surprise. Are you coming?" When the man had lived upstairs, the boy's mother had told him never to bother him.

The earliest thing the boy remembered was darkness, what he thought was the darkness from when he'd been born, and in the darkness distant music and after that, the next thing was a man in brown standing on the staircase to the third floor, looking down at him.

The boy had been three years old and he was in the hall looking up at Mr. Spizarsky as the man descended past the second floor on his way to work. Mr. Spizarsky had had the room on the third floor since 1949 when he'd come in on the train from Halifax, leaving everything behind him with no future and no past, a moving line of the present like the band on the dial of a radio. He had taught the philosophy of time to gymnasia students, bright adolescents in Cracow. As the train pulled into Union Station, in Toronto, he had stood up, drawn a cigarette from a silver cigarette case given him by his uncle, the uncle that had disappeared. He lit the cigarette, got his shoes polished, oiled and combed back his hair in the mirror over the seat, the gold tooth glinting in sunlight. He brushed his hat and put on cologne with a dab in his breast pocket handkerchief. In his right hand pocket he still carried the straight razor, had carried it for protection when he had walked from Cracow to Lisbon through a Europe that didn't exist anymore. He was a classicist. His papers were in order. In his inside pocket was a letter from Luba with a return address in East Germany, now under the shadow of Stalin. Her brown eyes, her bratty smile. He would write her when he had a proper address and when she arrived, that was when the future would start.

He emerged on Front Street. He carried two suitcases, the larger for his personal effects and the good blue suit made by a Jew in Prague. The brown suit which he wore had been made in Lyon. In the smaller case was proof of what had happened, in the event that nobody believed him.

He took a cheap hotel room on Queen Street; the architecture looked temporary, ornate, chaotic, jumbled with electric wires and advertising. He ate in a diner. The food was shit. He got a cleaning job at a bowling alley on Spadina. The girls were in bars or on street corners at night. They had no proper establishments here, no etiquette. He took a girl to his hotel room. She was fair, he paid her, went out to the washroom. When he came back, she was looking inside the small suitcase, claimed it had been lying open and she was shocked, it was disgusting, horrible. He told her to mind her own business, smacked her, shoved her out, almost threw her down the stairs, combed his hair back in the mirror, his hair sleek, dark eyes, cigarette, looked like Valentino, a ladies' man. Of course that would change when Luba got here. He was a classicist. He was in his mid-forties but she was ten years younger, they would have children. They would move to the suburbs where everything was new under wide blue skies and the war would be in the past.

The boy set up his soldiers in his room then ran downstairs and rode on the old housekeeper's floor polisher as she sang "You are my sunshine..." He looked at his distorted reflection in the silver on the sideboard, went out to the garden, raced his wagon around, ran in again. In the afternoon a white truck came by, jangling immense music with important talking on a loudspeaker. His mother got him ice cream and the music went away and it was the distant music he'd heard in the dark at the beginning. It always went away into the west, far behind the house to the purple where the sun set, where he would go one day. At bedtime he went to the window to see what happened to the sun, where it went down, and the harder he looked the farther away and stranger it seemed.

An Italian in the bowling alley put Mr. Spizarsky onto a job with a Polish butcher in Kensington. Mr. Spizarsky had worked for his uncle who'd been a butcher outside Cracow and his father had been a cattle dealer. Both had disappeared. Kensington was a little like a market in Galicia, a hint of what once had been but second-rate. And really a lot of Jews, a lot of bearded Hasidim. He took a room in Kensington and worked carrying meat. He wanted to teach classics. He slept badly but there was nothing but noise here, delivery trucks all night. He was wakened by the least sound but it was getting back to sleep that brought the thing that was more than darkness, it was full of something, like flesh, inaudible words, dirty water, filth, following you with force which increased until it was overwhelming and would annihilate you and then just silence and a squeaking sound, like a sign pole in the wind. He needed quiet. He bought some undershirts from a Hungarian place on Augusta in Kensington, asked where he could get a room in a decent, quiet neighbourhood. The Hungarian sent him to his cousin, Andrew Molnar on Warwick Avenue.

North of Bloor was different, heavy trees, big old solid houses, separate, with alleys and gardens. And dead quiet. Molnar was an old guy; he'd come because of the Russians. A big three-storey brick house full of family and relatives. His wife made borscht and goulash. Molnar made wine in the basement. Spizarsky rented a small room on the second floor, like home in a way. It took a while to remember when he had last had a home. He and Molnar got drunk on Molnar's wine down in the basement. Neither missed the old country. The only thing he missed, oddly, was Grimm's fairy tales, fairy tales which he had always imagined happening in the countryside of the Galicia of his childhood.

He would have to improve his English to teach. Kinski, the butcher, was treating him like a goddamn serf, the man didn't even know who Dostoevsky was. He told Kinski to go fuck himself and got work down at the Texaco station on the corner of Warwick and Bathurst and mowed lawns up the street for a Ukrainian woman. He ate down at the Hungarian restaurants on Bloor, wiener schnitzel, goulash, drank at a social club with a bunch of other Poles, Ukrainians, Rumanians; they all lied about the war, about what had happened. He kept his mouth shut, got drunk. He paid for girls out by Roncesvalles. He more or less had a job and now an address for Luba. He wrote her telling her to come. She was the only thing left in the world that he loved.

Everything was suspended.

Molnar said his nephew was coming from Hungary and he needed the room but people up the street had a room for rent, Canadians. That was what he wanted. He wanted to know real Canadians, the blue sky and the future. He knocked. Mr. and Mrs. Hart asked him in, told him to sit down. He took a straight-backed chair inside the door, kept his reserve. They talked. At least they had a little culture. Their kid came into the room, a three-year-old. The kid would grow up with money, knowing nothing about the world, about the kind of thing that could happen. Spizarsky drew a cigarette from the silver cigarette case.

Mrs. Hart, who read much of the day, found Mr. Spizarsky rakish and worldly wise with beautiful manners; she was impressed that he knew the works of Dostoevsky. Spizarsky was curious that Mr. Hart worked in advertising. A vulgar business but it was the future and the money was good. They also knew about the Austro-Hungarian Empire. He said he considered himself a Pole first, Galician second; they had left the Empire in 1918. They chatted about the war. Mr. Hart had fought with the Canadian army on the Western Front. He said, "I guess you must have had a time of it on the east, eh?"

Spizarsky had the northeast bedroom on the third floor, a front dormer and a side window north onto an alley and blue sky that he swore was the future. The room was quiet. He sent Luba the new address. In a few weeks he dropped in at Molnar's and still, she hadn't written. The dream bothered him less now; instead, he'd started to think about the bomb, Stalin; these people and the Americans did not know what they had gotten themselves into, they were fools. One morning, on the way to the gas station, he had just lit a cigarette and was coming down from the third floor when he stopped, checking to see if he'd left his keys, noticing the little kid, Henry, below, staring up at him.

The man on the stairs in a brown suit with a cigarette looked strange as he continued on down. The man never spoke and his door was always closed. The man came from the blue smoke and cloud where the sun went down, which was also in the pages of the book his father read to him, a book that you could open all the way round and tie with a ribbon with cut-out scenes like a carousel of royal courts, enchanted forests and stone battlements with a sleeping sky without time. That was where he'd go as soon as they let him play out in front.

Sometimes he ran up to the third floor to play in the spare room where there were piles of books and he gazed at the covers of Signet paperbacks, the red-lipped swooning blonde women, the shadows of a man in a brown suit and fedora, the man in the next room. Once the man's door was ajar, a grubby, forbidden world of shadows and bottles and there was a roar, "Kid, get the hell out of there, get out!" and rearing up from the stairs, the man yelled and the boy ran down the stairs, his heart hammering.

The next day Spizarsky put a padlock on the door and Mr. Hart said to Mrs. Hart, "He didn't even inquire and it looks like crap, like a rooming house." Mr. Hart had a proper lock put on the door, and gave Mr. Spizarsky the key.

Spizarsky began to notice that the quiet there had a certain emptiness. Mr. and Mrs. Hart had successfully petitioned to get the ice cream truck off their street. It was a danger to children and the music was a nuisance. Spizarsky thought they were ridiculous, keeping life at arm's length, when you could still hear it two streets over, fading westward. The silence and control in this city was apparently Protestant. Mr. Hart had invited him for a drink only once and that had been when Mr. Hart had himself been drunk and come home late on a hot summer night. They had sat out on the back veranda, drinking scotch, and Mr. Hart had talked about fighting in Antwerp, the horrors of war. He still seemed surprised by it, baffled that everything wasn't like Canada. As Mr. Hart talked about seeing entire rivers of rats in Berlin, Spizarsky recalled kissing Luba for a long time before he put her into a honking car with a suitcase in the middle of a blackened plain and the smell of burnt flesh, and the car diminished toward a wall of fire. They would be in Bautzen, Germany, staying with her in-laws; he still had the scrawled address on a crumpled piece of paper. Of the time before that day there remained nothing, it was a place of darkness. Sometimes he was no longer even sure what had been there. Ages had passed and still, he had not heard from Luba.

He came home from work and said hello to Gene, the neighbour. Gene was from somewhere in Eastern Europe with horn-rimmed glasses and a grey brush cut, pleasant and cheerful but would never say what country he was from, would only speak English. He wondered what Gene knew. As Spizarsky went upstairs, the television murmured, a world of idiocy.

Henry was watching *Howdy Doody*. He watched Lestoil commercials, Tide commercials, *Popeye*, detective movies, images of palm trees, guns, detectives, cars, rain, the city at night, ships in port, all of it in the west, beyond, in the western sky, where the sleeping sky of the castle was, where Mr. Spizarsky went, adventure, the world, grenadiers; in the sunset, where the music had gone.

Spizarsky sat on the bed, lit a cigarette, turned on the radio. He was in a rut. He had dance partners at the social club. Slovenians, Croats, Ukrainians, Polish. If you touched them, you had to buy them dinner, if you bought dinner, they wanted marriage. Getting to fuck them had become a chore. He tried to stop seeing the women at Queen and Roncesvalles, the chaos of streetcar wires, cheap hotels, the bus depot. The business with women seemed so secret, illicit in this country. He had returned to Mass, the priest, the chasuble, the raised chalice, the only thing that was the same as Poland, he confessed to the priest and occasionally confessed about the women. At the social club, where he hardly went now, he'd heard about a woman on College, a Ukrainian. She was more civilized, established, like they had been in Galicia, where there had been houses where you went into a parlour and you chose from women sitting around a table. This woman, Katerina, had her own place. He went down there, a second-floor walk-up. She was good-looking. Doilies, curtains, lace, flowers, like at home. She gave him tea. Her husband had disappeared during the Nazi retreat, was later reported dead. They talked about the old country, the other world from before 1941 and she gave him dinner. They went into the bedroom and he paid her. She was a little expensive but she knew who Dostoevsky was, she knew about Sobieski and Poniatowsky. It made waiting for Luba easier.

When he got home after work, coming up into the second-floor hall and turning toward the third-floor stairs, he noticed Henry down in the end room on the floor with lead soldiers, British grenadiers, knocking them over with marbles. Children should be told about goddamn militarism, what it led to. He unlocked his room, from nowhere the thought of suicide but then it was gone.

Henry heard the voices of the girls and ran to the window. He had heard Wendy and Karen talk about where the music went. They had been there. Their faces were chalky, grey, they smelled of dirt, sometimes they mentioned their mother but it seemed they never had to be home, he didn't know which house they lived in, someone had said they lived in a basement. They said the word "Christie" about the streets after you went around the block, the streets that were farther. He went down. He was allowed to play on the front lawn now. He'd never been around the block where the west was, where the evening was. He wasn't allowed past the corner. Judy just laughed and asked him what was wrong. Wendy and Karen and Judy said they were going over to Christie and asked him why he didn't want to come. He was nervous and went with them around the first corner but at the second corner he turned back. At bedtime, he asked his father to read the fold-out book but they couldn't find it, though his father swore he had left it to one side on the third-floor stairs. They read another book, *Children of the World*. After his light was turned out he played a game; he'd listen for the distant music in the dark until he thought he heard it. And it always came.

In the morning, Spizarsky walked down to the gas station, the green lawns, the white porches. When the bomb fell it would start all over again, these people knew nothing. It had come fast then too, first with motorbikes, for a moment he'd thought it was the police, the Nazis had come so quickly, and it all seemed to happen in silence. They took all the key places and started killing people without fuss; he'd figured it was the fucking Saxon minority who had invited them in. At first the Nazis were after Jews. He'd seen two children and their mother come out of a kosher butcher. Two officers stepped out of a staff car, asked the mother for her papers, one pulled his pistol and shot her and the children on the spot. People went on shopping. On the way to his father's place, after teaching, he saw rows of dead Jews, adults and children, shot by the road. When they started killing other people he began to wonder about having a Jewish grandfather, and then people were hanging by wire from shop signs, good Galician Catholics like himself, suspected of concealing Jews. He didn't like Jews but still there were good Jews and bad Jews, except now his brother and his sister had been interrogated and he had the feeling that sooner or later he'd see them swinging from shop signs. He knew a Jewish butcher who had cheated his father in a livestock deal. He walked into the town hall and told a Gestapo man behind a typewriter everything he knew. They took the man away. Once the Nazis trusted him, he was able to protect Schlieffman, the Jewish watchmaker, a decent Jew, who had made watches for his father and grandfather. He had the feeling there'd been others he'd protected or sold, but it was murky, his memory had gotten shaky. He had one of his uncle's meat trucks. The Germans ordered him to use it to distribute their propaganda sheet, *Achtung!* It featured photographs of what the Gestapo did to people who didn't cooperate. If he refused, he knew what they would do to his brother and his brother's wife.

He sat on the bed in his undershirt, had a smoke, a glass of Szekszardi wine, cheap but all right, read the Polish paper, the smaller suitcase sitting closed on the straight-backed chair. He had not opened it, had not looked at its contents since leaving Europe, nine years ago. He'd heard nothing from Luba. He turned on the radio, listened to Tchaikovsky. He had studied the violin when he was young, in Cracow. It reminded him of children, of being in a room with little girls, their soft white arms and legs, their fine hair, he felt like being surrounded by children, girls, to get rid of what had happened, he imagined the little girls from across the street, drove it from his mind. He had written Luba three times, had written to others, no one knew anything. So much could have happened. Once or twice he got into a stupid trap, a spiral, and thought of just taking the razor.

Mr. Hart said very quietly to Mrs. Hart, even though they were on the first floor, that the Ratepayers were getting on everyone's back about roomers. He was making money and now Henry would need his own room. They spoke to Spizarsky. Spizarsky thanked them for everything, packed and left.

After dinner, Henry stayed out later now, playing with the children in the street. Now he followed them beyond the two corners, running for blocks to keep up until they got to a big square park in a valley. He thought they'd been chasing the music and he was on the edge of the valley and the west was grey and purple and the music was in the distance, triumphant and elegiac and he watched the crowds in the dusk, the shining street light and chrome and the sky which had turned green in the incredible light and the others were gone and the stars were coming out and the music stayed there in the distance, it didn't go away, and he stood on his toes, his shoes were scuffed, his hands were dirty, he was a man in the thumping, racing excitement of the world, the whole world and beyond.

Spizarsky had been mowing the lawn of the old Hungarian lady two doors up, on the other side of Gene, so now he rented a room there. She did his laundry, gave him goulash and borscht. Her house was so clean it was sterile. But she hardly ever spoke and it began to worry him. He wondered why Gene next door spoke to him in English but would never say where in Eastern Europe he was from. The house was a similar house to the Harts' and his room was the same, northeast on the third floor, as if something were freezing everything, preventing him from moving on. After a long time it appeared that Luba and her family had been killed by the Communists or some family vendetta; either way, it seemed to be no man's land where she'd ended up, maybe a killing zone. Or maybe they were in Siberia. He'd found himself thinking of Katerina anyway. Except she was starting to be a problem now. He was in love with her.

In the room, after he'd waken in the night and fall back asleep, the dream came back: darkness, reddish chaos except now there were forms of streets drained of colour, nocturnal, sign poles, shapes hanging, drifting, the rhythmic squeak of rope and wire in the wind. He'd waken, light a cigarette.

Henry was driving up to get his tricycle fixed, the wheel was squeaking loudly. He rode fast, pretending there was a repair place at the corner, turned back at the corner, down to the house then up again. The man who'd been upstairs came out of the house two doors up in his undershirt with an oil can, smoking a cigarette. The boy's heart beating, he got off the tricycle, tried to stop from crying. The man laughed, took the tricycle and oiled the wheel. "This is what you do," he said and went back. Even on Saturday morning you couldn't sleep, sooner or later he would crack.

He didn't want to pay Katerina anymore. He'd become ashamed of it. He'd proposed marriage twice and she'd said nothing. She wouldn't even say no, she just sat there. He had a feeling there was something she wasn't telling him. He was drinking more now. Because of the heat, he and the next-door neighbour Gene would drink at three in the morning on their front porches, standing, talking across the partition, concealing the bottles.

He had needed Luba to keep going, to leave it all behind, the darkness, all that had and at the same time had not happened, now he needed Katerina, he could not be alone anymore, the sleeping, the waking, the roadsides, everything on fire, destroyed by the Germans from the west, razed by the Russians from the east, ruins, fields of charred corpses, fire, Reds machine-gunning disarmed Nazis by the hundred; then they started on everyone else, looked for collaborators with the Nazis, his chance to get back at the Germans, he gave them Nazi stragglers and a family of Saxons; a Nazi soldier he recognized, last out with a rearguard unit, packing up a field radio, he pretended to ask the man a question, flicked open the razor, cut the Nazi's throat, the warm animal blood on his hands, Toronto, lawns, sun, white porches and foraging food in ruins, when he came home on his lunch hour the building next door was gone, the strange silence of four Russians raping his sister Anna, her wide-eyed terror, and the next day the family house was gone, thought of Luba, people roaming like animals, none of this had been written, hunger, starved corpses, rib cages, everyone against everyone, Galician Poles hanging Galician Ukrainian Nazis with wire, a dirty thin child sitting on the ground eating pieces of a cat, flames, darkness, pigs eating the dead, blue sky outside his room, clean brick, houses, the street, sun and trees, children, television, people eating human remains, it had not been written, in shells of buildings, the only thing not being killed was Jews because there weren't any left, they'd all been taken away to Belzec and gassed in big halls when they thought they were only going to be deloused. Even the watchmaker, why did they have to kill the watchmaker, easy to turn your back because you'd been driven crazy, he'd killed someone, maybe others in darkness, so what? Grab your suitcases, new life, Luba in a Communist zone, writing letters, it will all end, riding in the backs of trucks, head lice, camps, Luba, holding centres, big healthy Americans in crisp uniforms, Luba, he rode a refugee train to Prague, money from the UNRRA, Luba, shifting from place to place, jobs for years, walk to France, to Portugal with a handful of stamped papers. Luba is gone. 1957. He still shaved with that fucking razor. Why? Who was he? Where?

The boy in his new bedroom, the dormer alcove, the side window, stripped clean to the walls as if Mr. Spizarsky had never been there, his toys on the shelf, his bed, sitting on the bed with the book *Children of the World*: John, the American, a cowboy; Ling, Chinese in the conical sun hat; Pierre, the Frenchman with a beret; Elena from Poland in an embroidered skirt; Ivan from Russia, boots and fur hat; Mohammed from Iran, sheepskin hat and coat, all with different countrysides, he wanted to see them where the sun went down, where the music was, ran downstairs, out the front door, into the alley, got on his tricycle, raced up the walk, China, Iran, deep shadows, trees and sunlight, the heat, Dolly the horse and the milk wagon, he passed Mr. Spizarsky, rode on up to the corner, hands sweating on rubber grips.

A heat wave. Lying naked with Katerina, damp bodies cooled in a slow breeze through billowing curtains. She had said she loved him too but still he had to pay her and still she wouldn't say anything. That night, in heavy heat, he stood on the front porch in his undershirt, chatting with Gene over the partition, the hiss of a gentle rain, the red embers of their cigarettes. He had a bottle of wine, Gene was drinking beer, three in the morning. He figured out Gene had known the things he'd known but they only talked about organizations, names, dates. And in English. With the rain and mist and darkness it could be Cracow and Luba both dead and alive, everything reconciled. He poured more wine.

A grey morning. Henry was a taxi driver with Wendy standing on the back of the tricycle, leaning on his shoulders. She said Spizarsky had taken them in and shown them scenes from *Beauty and the Beast* on the lady's front stairs. Henry told her he was a taxi, he could take her anywhere. He knew the whole world, he could take her to all the houses, to Iran, he could take her west to the park. Karen said it was the land of no return.

After work, Spizarsky went down to College, up the dark stairway, the air stale with the heat. He knocked and there was no answer. Katerina had agreed on six o'clock. He went down and asked the woman behind the counter in the dry cleaners. She said, Katerina's husband was alive, he had come to Canada. The woman was overjoyed for her. Katerina's dream had come true.

He went to a bar. The sun, the heat in drunkenness, the shadow, the gas station, the room, the window, the blue sky. The razor lay on his bedside table. On Monday, after work, he bought wine. The wine blurred everything together, the room, the darkness, the squeak of the kid's tricycle, the voices of the girls, their laughter. He went downstairs.

He stood in his undershirt, swaying a little, at the foot of the walk. They were jumping and squealing, he might even get them upstairs, girls, the warmth, they were the future, there was nothing more. The kid came up on his tricycle, wide clear blue eyes like glass staring up at him; fine, the kid, Henry, he could come too.

"You name the story, you get another surprise," he said. The street swam, he felt nothing.

Henry wanted to be with the girls. The girls knew everything. They had gone even farther into the sunset than he had, where the music was.

"Are you coming?" they kept saying. "Are you coming up?"

He was scared.

"Are you coming?" they said, jumping.

The stairs, everything was dark, dark flowers on the wall, the carpet, plastic flowers, the heavy smell of cooking. They kept going up and up, their feet thundering on the stairs and then into a room just like his room except it was hot and it smelled. The man told them all to sit on the bed. The man had a book just like the one his father read to him with the cut-out paper scenes and the sleeping sky without time. The man told them the story, scene by scene. He smelled, his breath smelled, his hair smelled. He closed the book and asked them to name it. *"Beauty and the Beast,"* Judy said. "Very good," he said, and they jumped and yelled and clapped. "Here is the first part of your prize," he said, and he gave them all candies. Henry got a yellow candy and an orange one. He wanted to go home. "And here is the other part," the man said, and he pulled over the smaller case and opened it.

The children looked. They bent to look closer. Photographs. Henry thought it was pictures of dolls. The man opened more pages of the yellowed newspaper, in fairy tale gothic writing, *Achtung!* to more photographs, and there was a scream, the boy didn't know why and then he knew and he didn't know and there was crying, faces, dark, distortion, eye holes, broken stained doll heads, things dirty and smashed, no one said what it was, it was and it wasn't, the room filled with screaming and they went down the stairs crying and he cried too, it spread to the flowered walls and even the street and he ran.

The sun slanted through the window, late and intense. Spizarsky started to fall asleep.

A few days later, the boy was having his supper when he heard his parents in the living room saying that something had happened to Mr. Spizarsky. The boy went up and watched *Davy Crockett* on television. After he went to bed and his mother turned out the light, the boy listened for the distant music in the dark and he kept listening, but now there was nothing, only the dark.

YOU MAY AS WELL COME DOWN

The boy was eight years old when he first saw them materializing out of the mist: a bantam-sized old man in a small straw hat and a giant lumbering man almost as old. Later, the boy's father introduced him to them and the boy was afraid of them because they had bad grammar and looked at him as if they were about to laugh and teased him about getting up late and said a man who got up late never got anywhere. They had big noses and missing teeth and each had a deep abscess scar in his cheek, which gave a look of wild inhaling. The boy's father later told him that the big man, the son, was subnormal. The boy would remember them as smelling of damp cloth and mildew and something he couldn't name, and it was only a long time afterward that he realized they had smelled of death. The year was 1963.

The boy's name was Henry and his parents had just bought the farm where he first saw the two men. During the week, his father worked fifty miles away in Toronto. Henry's older brother had been sent to school abroad. Now, at the farm, his mother wrote articles on foreign affairs and talked on the telephone. So Henry watched television. To Henry, the country seemed dry and dead. He wanted to be back in the city, but his mother kept telling him to play outside and finally he went out.

At first it looked like nothing, like wreckage. There was a feeling of oldness: in the paintless barn, in the rusted pieces of implements and harness; in the panic of pigeons that blew up when he entered the loft, their diaphanous passage across the cracks of light; in the shit, the dust and the decay rising like acrid smoke in the strips of light. He found pieces of enamel-ware that people must have eaten and drunk out of. And outside, in the field, he found bones. He did not know whether they were animal bones, but he imagined them as human bones from disinterments at midnight.

At lunch one day his mother went on about why he didn't draw or read or use his imagination, and reminded him that his friends were ahead of him. About to cry, he ran outside. He wasn't supposed to go near the highway, but he ran across the road and went up the sloping fields. There was an abandoned house on a ridge, and by the time he got there he was scratched by barbed wire and tall-standing weeds, and even though it looked smaller close up, the house seemed suddenly dangerous. But he couldn't go back, so he pushed at the door until it gave. Inside he found an old edition of *The Wizard of Oz* torn and scattered across the floor on top of some girls' dresses, all of it covered with bird shit, and the plaster fallen from the laths, the panes gone from the windows. He found a medicine cabinet with bottles inside that said 1926 and a tin of brilliantine still marked by fingertips, and overalls hanging on the wall. He looked around upstairs and when he came down he heard someone shout, and when he went out the door he saw a red-faced man in overalls yelling and the man fired a shotgun and the boy went running through high weeds as a charge of salt whizzed past his legs.

He was afraid that if he told his parents, they would talk to the red-faced man, so he said nothing. It was around then that the two old men started coming. The older man's name was Mr. Beedon and the son was named Alf and they came in an old black 1949 Dodge to cut cedar fence posts. Henry's father was renting out pasture for grazing and the old man, Beedon, was going to help replace the fencing. They were talking to Henry's father about distances in chains and rods. After a silence the big man, Alf, said solemnly, "Craggshaws stole timber off this place once," and spat absently through the gap in his teeth. The old man looked at him, his toothless mouth a moment agonized, and snapped, "That's enough out of you, you don't know what you're talking about." When Alf continued, the old man sharply kicked him in the shin. "We won't hear no more out of you," he said. And Alf nodded silently as if to affirm what he'd managed to say. Henry wondered who the Craggshaws were.

A few days later he was playing in a field beyond the barn, wielding a stick as a sword and attacking an army of milk-weed. He turned and saw standing behind him a boy, a couple of years older, slouching with a rifle cradled in his forearm, the heel of one foot in the instep of the other, like the photograph of Billy the Kid. There was no wind and the sky behind him was even grey like a tintype. He said he'd been hunting ground-hogs in their long field and spoke slowly and formally, disclosing that he knew the day Henry and his family had arrived there; who had owned the property back three generations;

that twenty years ago a child had died falling into a well on that property, and there were things in the area Henry's family would never know about. Henry thought of the name Craggshaw and looked at the boy and the boy went off and Henry went back to the milkweed and turned and the boy was gone out of thin air.

On Sunday night Henry's father was leaving for the city when he told the boy that he was to help the old man put in fence posts and that it would make a man of him. Henry lay awake that night thinking of the toothless abscess scars and the faded smell; of Beedon's pale eyes that seemed to see through everything and of the old man kicking his son.

In the morning Beedon took him out to the boundary line. The old man sighted the fence line and told Henry to shift the crowbar until it was in line. Beedon marked the ground and lifted the sod with the shovel and dug the hole. They began to put the posts in and the boy was pounding in the dirt when there was a shout, a bark: "What the Sam Hill have you done! Look! Looka that!" The boy had trampled half the dirt back into the grass so that the old man had to scrape it back to fill in the post. His eyes were wild with outrage and he said if there wasn't enough earth to fill it up level the rain would get in and rot the wood in seven instead of fifteen years and the fence would be down and cattle would get out and destroy a crop and there would be a lawsuit.

Later Henry saw the old man staring at a great elm tree. He predicted that it would survive the elm disease. Then he said there was an elm tree down in Goodwood that was so big it yielded forty cords of firewood. Later that afternoon he said that in 1931 he had won a bet estimating the height of the tallest church spire in the township.

The following day the boy watched while Beedon used an axe-head to make machine-perfect notches in the anchor posts for the brace poles as he named the local farmers who had cheated him out of wages. He named the few people in the area who were "all right" and the majority who were "no good." He told the boy of people committed to the insane asylum at Whitby, of a barn fire that he was sure was arson, of the daughter of a storekeeper who had died drinking muriatic acid, of a butcher who had hanged himself.

For several days they worked, the old man talking on as if to himself. He began to stretch the wire, levering each strand taut with a crowbar, one leg raised with the strain while the boy hammered, terrified of bending the staples. When it seemed he was doing it right, Henry asked how the village had been started. After a moment the old man said, "Craggshaws." The boy wondered why they would have stolen wood from the lot, but said nothing and then Beedon said, "They come from up by Leith originally. People said they were no good." Henry had driven near there with his father. It was in a stark plain off the highway a few miles north of the village, a place where you could see a four-storey hotel from miles away. The old man said that long ago Craggshaws were the cause of a lot of trouble, but much of what people said about them was lies.

"What kind of trouble?" Henry said.

"They were always fightin'. Fightin' all the time...You didn't want to get in trouble with them." Then he paused and muttered, "They run the township at one time."

The fence was soon done. The old man was gone. At the end of August the boy and his parents returned to Toronto. Henry's mother told him they'd be going up there on weekends. Henry's brother Tom was home for Christmas and then went back to Switzerland. Henry felt alone again but now he didn't like the city. He looked forward to the country. The Beedons had no telephone, and when Henry and his parents drove up, they took a long detour on some side roads to ask if Beedon and his son could come on Saturday to cut firewood. On the way, Henry heard his parents remarking that Beedons had been there for eighty-odd years and didn't seem to have a single friend in the area. His mother wondered if they'd been ostracized.

Henry was nervous about going into their house because his mother had told him they were poor. They reached a high bare ridge and skidded down a snowbound lane and went up onto the veranda of a stone house and were let in by Beedon's wife, twisted and beaky like an ancient bird in men's shoes and with glasses held together with tape. There was a blast of dry heat from a wood stove and in the one room where they lived the wallpaper was torn and water stained. The old man, bald and white and without his hat, sat in a rocker and Alf watched television, drinking beer, and the old woman sat and stared with her arms folded and the room smelled of that same dank oldness. This is not now, Henry thought, this is then. This is how it was; and it's still here, in this strange light in this house high on this hill at night.

~ ~ ~

The following June, at the farm, Beedon put in the gardens and the vegetable patch and Henry ran and got things for him. After a while he noticed the old man standing, his hands on his hips, looking down and thinking, then he muttered something about cutting thistles and said, "You may as well come down." The old man didn't need the boy's help but he wanted him along, and it was then that Henry thought, I'm one of them, and realized only later that "them" were the dead, the inhabitants of the old man's world, the gone world. The land was dry and dusty, and the sky was purple-black over the village and there was fork lightning and the starlings were crowded along the telephone lines and the branches hung dusty and still, and when Beedon began to talk as he swung the scythe, the air was pregnant with something terrible.

He worked with the old man every day now. As Beedon cut wood and cleared thistles and mused aloud, half to himself, the boy learned that he had rented and lived and worked at twenty-seven houses in that one county over sixty-odd years. He had had thirty-four employers. Small as he was, he had won fights over girls outside dance halls in 1906 and 1910 at places that had once been crossroads and now were weedy outlines in fields. He had been the only one who could lift a full-grown heifer into the back of a wagon. And he mentioned names: names he had worked for; names with whom he had fought over the price of fence wire, over wages; names he had accused of inexplicable acts of malice.

At the end of the week some friends of Henry's mother arrived from England and they were having tea and she wanted Henry to be there, and she was calling him, but he went on up the hill and joined the old man, who was stringing barbed wire. Again, Beedon began to talk. He talked of various people he had worked for who told him of place after place that had burned, and he murmured, "Of course, that was the time of the arson, there."

"What's arson?" the boy said.

The old man looked at him and said, "Settin' fires," then added, "There were six Craggshaw sons; a few of them were all right but the rest were no good."

"Did you know them?" the boy asked.

The old man paused and withdrew the wire stretcher and moved on. "I knew a couple of them, but never no trouble with them, not really. Most of it happened round when I was born."

"When were you born?"

"I was born in 1879," Beedon said.

~ ~ ~

The following day the boy was with him when he was hoeing the tomatoes, and the old man said that as far as the Craggshaws were concerned, one thing was true: they had higher yields than anyone could explain. They even bought the two three-storey hotels in Leith that stood across the street from each other and still loomed in a single black block on the horizon. But in his opinion it was Bascombs who were the worst. Bascombs were the oldest and biggest landowners in the area and after Craggshaws arrived, that was when the arson started. Hooligans used it as an excuse and the hotel saloons were nicknamed "the buckets of blood" and both hotels were gutted by arson.

Beedon broke for lunch and Henry went in and put the lunch his mother had made into a plastic bread bag like the bag Beedon brought his lunch in, then went into the driving shed and sat by him on the sill beam. The boy asked him why the Craggshaws were so bad and the old man squinted out into the light.

"They had somethin', somethin' about them," he said. "I don't know what it was." He said they had wit; they had the best women, the best coaches, the best harness and the best clothes and "everybody had something" to say about them. But it wasn't just that, it was something "else." It sounded like something evil and knowing that still resided behind wallpaper and warped walls in old houses.

"And then there was more trouble and they killed them one night," Beedon said. "They killed most of them, anyway. It was in the winter of '81."

"Where?" Henry said.

"Up by Leith," he said. "I was – Gol – I was two years old, I guess."

"Why did they kill them?"

"They say Bascombs done it," and he told the boy about being taken into Leith by his father a few years afterward and his father pointing out the notorious Willy Bascomb laughing and trying to make a horse kick in front of the post office. And there was still the fear, but by then it was fear of Bascombs, not of Craggshaws.

"People sold and moved out," he said, "because of the murders and the burnings." And then in 1895, they diverted the railroad and a few years later they put in a highway five miles east and that was the end of Leith. The town that had once domi-nated the countryside shrank to nothing and it was as if noth-ing had happened there.

It felt to the boy like a secret, and when he overheard his parents talking about how much time he spent with the old man he wanted to tell them to mind their own business. It seemed to interest them the way the markings on finches or Roman bronzes did and he swore he would never interest them anymore and they would never know his world. He would not even tell his brother Tom.

A few days later his mother said to him that Beedon had asked if, instead of paying him for finishing the zucchini patch, Henry could help him on a job near the village of Purdew. Henry's heart beat faster, because Purdew was near Leith.

"I'll talk to him about it," Henry said offhandedly and that made his mother laugh and he hid his fury. This job made him one of them, side by side with the old man and Alf.

~ ~ ~

They went in Alf's car several miles north of the village to the land that was flat by a crossroads, and the remaining hotel was still large and stark. Leith was a cracked asphalt detour and wizened main street off the highway, with a garage, a couple of stores overgrown with weeds, and the old hotel dominating the shrunken country. They turned onto a side road, a tired vec-tor over flat fields that looked old, and they slowed at a lane. Two boys idled on bicycles. When they turned, one of the boys cut slowly across in front of them, and the paleness of his face and the humped boniness of his back made Henry think of milk out of a barn a long time ago, and both boys rode close to the windows and said something as the car drove in along the lane.

The car went through alfalfa to a fence that went to the horizon, and a man called Purvis, who had lost part of his nose, showed them where the fence was down and his cattle had got into an infant cemetery that was abandoned and overgrown. They set up an electric battery, and Beedon said the children had died because of bad well water. The land was so flat that it seemed to Henry that the children had been killed by the weight of the sky. It was different here; there was an immensity. There was power and sadness.

They strung the electric wire in silence. There was no wind now. As if he were picking up where he had left off, but again talking to himself, Beedon said that the Bascombs had had so much influence that those who had killed the Craggshaws were found not guilty.

"But that one brother knew who did it," Alf said.

As if his son had not spoken, Beedon said that one Craggshaw, Robert, was absent from the house on the night of the murders, and years later a Justice of the Peace gave Robert Craggshaw some papers that would have convicted Willie Bascomb and the rest of them. Alf nodded. The crickets were deafening and the old man said that when Robert Craggshaw died in 1911 no one knew where he had kept the papers. But Beedon thought the papers were still in Craggshaw's house.

Alf said, "On the eighth line of Victoria there," and the old man shouted at him, "There's nobody in it now anyway, you—!" and sent Henry back out to the road to flag down a truck delivering fence posts.

The two boys were there, idling on bicycles. They were older than he was, with big pale muscles. It was all theirs: the white dust, the heavy roadside grass, the fences, the distance. He tried to stare back at them and they said something and he heard them laugh. A stone sailed slowly past his head and he knew that what they were doing was old and worse because of it. The sky was now wan, the sky after a calamity, yet too vast to have changed so quickly. A fast stone hit him in the shoulder and the truck came down the road and Henry raised his hand and went into the lane. Stones whipped past his head and he had to run behind the truck.

When the work was done and the old men and the boy came out to the road, the older boys were still there in the twilight and staring again, and in their faces, half obliterated by the darkness, the boy saw the thickness of ninety years. Beedon and Alf knew who they were and they went toward the Dodge and a pebble bounded off the hood and Alf turned back toward them, rolling up his sleeve like a cartoon brawler and the boys rode slowly away as Alf said, "Mallen boys." In the car, the fields passed in darkness and Alf said there was a Bascomb in the mental hospital in Whitby who was supposed to have sworn that if he ever got out he'd burn the Craggshaw house to the ground because of the papers that were there. Beedon told him not to say what he didn't know.

~ ~ ~

For a while Beedon only came to cut the grass. Henry was watching *Sea Hunt* when his mother came upstairs and said he was watching television when he had agreed not to and there were shelves full of books downstairs. There was James Fenimore Cooper and *Alice in Wonderland* and Dickens, which she herself had started reading when she was younger than he was. His brother Tom had read them all and if Henry didn't start now, he would stay second-rate. It seemed he was the one thing that hadn't worked out in his parents' world of international travel, business and writing and life in the country, and after she left he squeezed his fist until it was white and he cried. It was still before dinner and he went out the back door.

He went up through the village and onto a side road that climbed the long slope to the ridge, and he kept walking, as if by walking far enough he would eventually have no connection with either of his parents and could say he was from somewhere else. He went up a lane and the land fell away in nameless violence into the twilight and he went to the stone house and an acre of cut grass and a few bleeding hearts and then the porch. Beedon's wife was there and she let him in. The old woman gave him supper and he watched television. Beedon came in and neither the old man nor the old woman said much to each other or to the boy and Henry watched *Gunsmoke* while Beedon ate.

The boy slept on a settee under coats. In the morning there was mist and he went out to the barn with the old man, and on the way there was a sweet manure and sour milking smell that felt remembered.

Then his father came and got him and on the way back gave him a reprimand, and at home his mother sat him down and explained at length that they had been upset only because they loved him. It was a love he didn't understand, did not even think much about, and a week later, when he saw the trail of black smoke going up on the horizon, he knew they could not see what he saw because it was from eighty years ago. He and Beedon had been down in the cedar bush where the old man was cutting burdocks and Alf had come to drive him home. Henry climbed into the car and they drove up to Leith. Before the side road with the infant cemetery there was an unpainted house at a weedy corner by the highway, devoured in smoke and fire. There were cars all along the shoulder and a crowd and they got out and walked along and Alf addressed several people who did not respond or even look at him and Beedon snapped at him to keep to himself. As they drove back, Henry asked how it had happened and Beedon murmured, "It was set."

When the boy got home he mentioned the fire to his mother but refused to say anything more, and went to his room and the smudge in the sky was still there in the distance, alive and present and fading the way the past was.

~ ~ ~

It was late summer and there was little work left for the old man to do and even though another spring would come, the boy feared never seeing the old man again. Henry's mother sent him up the hill to pick apples and he had begun to fill the basket when he saw the boy with the rifle again and he had his heel in his instep and the rifle cradled like before. And the sky was again grey, the grey of an old photograph, and there was that oldness and a sort of gone evil and the older boy spoke with slow formality and Henry said nothing and then there was just silence and the boy with the rifle said, "Likely the old fellow that works for you told you about it, eh?" They're still alive, Henry thought, they are still here among us.

"We don't talk about it," the boy with the rifle said. He squinted at Henry a long time and then said, "But that old man, he don't care. 'Cause all he was after was if you paid him good you were all right and he had less trouble with Bob Craggshaw over money and all that than he did with some other people." He went on speaking with a sort of slow, knowing vengeance. "I know he worked for Bob Craggshaw, ploughin' for him, nineteen-o-six, nineteen-o-nine when nobody else would because of what had happened and all. That's why he went up with you and his son to see the fire in Leith there, 'cause he knew it was Craggshaw's." The boy with the rifle had his chest out and his neck back like a fighting cock as if he owned the land and the past in some way, and said, "I know it was Jordie Bascomb done it. 'Cause he just come out of the mental hospital."

And Henry thought of the Bascomb who was afraid of the secret papers. "People won't talk to the old man Beedon 'cause he worked for Bob Craggshaw," the kid with the rifle said. "That's why them kids were throwin' stones at you over in Purdew. 'Cause they're Mallens." Then he went away.

~ ~ ~

In Toronto, in September, there were two worlds. There was the present world of school and his faltering marks and there was the world of the land fifty miles away, dead-still before a storm; of barns and lightning and the old man, always seen from behind: the baggy, indigo trousers and the 'Y' of his suspenders and the straw hat. And beyond him, infinity, haze receding into silence.

In November Henry arrived home from a friend's house, with the image of the old man, faceless, his arms out as if he were about to fight or as if he were holding an invisible plough, and the boy was sitting down to his milk and cookies in the kitchen when his mother came in looking in a way he had never seen her. At the office, his father had just had a heart attack and was now in Emergency. In the living room the boy sat beside her while she held her face in her hands, and then he sat on his bed thinking that he had never gotten to know his father and that if his father died, he never would. The following day after school he played ball hockey and did his homework and had supper at his friend's house and afterward they laughed hard at a show on television. He went home and found his mother on the telephone to his brother in Switzerland. His father had recovered; his father was fine, although he now had to be careful of his health.

In March the snow was almost gone and the trees were wet and black. He asked his mother when they were going up to the farm and she said, "I don't know. We may not be able to keep it. Because of your father's condition," and turned back to her typewriter. He went to the front door, opened it, kicked it as hard as he could and went out slamming it. When he came back at supper she said nothing except that what he had done was boorish and uncivilized and if there was something that bothered him he should say what it was. She added that they would have other places to go during the summer.

That spring his mother refused to talk about the farm; all she would say was that they would probably sell it. But for the time being, they wanted to see if there was any way of renting out more of the pasture. She was going to make inquiries and during Henry's Easter holidays they drove out to the country. When they got there the snow was not yet gone and the boy played in the fields and watched the mist rising out of the ground and the still dead pasture materialized as he had remembered it.

They had just had lunch and he was doing his homework when his mother got off the telephone and came in and paused and looked at him and said that she was sorry but that Beedon had died. The boy went out to the barn, and he went out to the pasture and it was still like the old man. He went up to his room, where he kept walking around and sitting down, and when he came down for dinner he couldn't eat. His mother told him he could stop from crying by distracting himself and she tried to hug him, but he pulled away and she told him that, if it was any help, they'd be coming back for at least half the summer.

On Sunday night they went back to the city. At school, at recess, he thought of running down into a nearby ravine because it was like the country and there were still ruined sections of farm fencing there, and then he thought of running away altogether. He didn't know where he would go, but he wanted to go into something, something ancient and absolute, a place as familiar and age-old as his own hand.

That fall, his parents sold the farm.

~ ~ ~

Four years later, when he was fourteen, he was in Coles when he saw a large illustrated book called *The Craggshaw Affair: The Photographic History, 1845-1890*. There were faces and fields and storefronts in decaying black-and-white and he recognized it, recognized the oldness. There were fragments of things that were still there in a landscape already as eaten-down and faded and rich with old corn as the country he had known. Many of the things in the book the old man had told him and many things he hadn't and there were things the old man had said that weren't in the book. But from something about the old man himself he recognized the satanic extravagance in the lapels and double-breasted waistcoats of the Craggshaw boys, as if the image had only sharpened. Then it would all fade and later would return again as dark and splendid as the rotted cloth and broken enamel and rusted wire he had found in stables and farmhouses, and the vicious grandeur of the people who had used them. And he read and re-read statements to a magistrate about Robert Craggshaw's attempted murder of a town constable and his beating of one of the Bascombs in that main street, once monumental and now small and vacant.

Sometimes, when he was on the verge of sleep or just waking, he saw the old man there. He was there in a land of crowded empty bottles and broken insulators, of dust and mildew and crumbling plaster; always facing away, just the "Y" of his suspenders and his small straw hat and beyond them both the darkening country; and the boy wanted to go after him into a world of thunder skies and arson and magnificence and living side roads. And Robert Craggshaw, who had once had twenty-eight charges of assault against him and nine

of arson, who had lived and fought at the same time as the out-
laws of the American West, would say to the old man in 1909,
"We've got to re-fence that whole part by the stream, I've
already had cattle through there and I don't want any trouble
now."

The boy would lie awake, seeing it over and over until the
grey pasture bleached into faded colour and light and all would
start to move and the old man would finally turn to him and say,
"You may as well come down." And Henry would go down
with them, he would go down with them to the pasture, forever.

THAT'S ALL THERE IS

Many houses on the street had once been mansions but were now broken into large apartments and rundown rooming houses. Henry lived in the biggest house, a corner mansion with wide dark windows that gave the impression of an old hotel. The apartment had high ceilings, with Regency and Victorian furniture. The brass and silver were always polished. There were shelves of books in every room and the television was in the study, all but concealed. These were the days when all the brick houses were still the colour of soot, before the renovators, when everyone still had coal furnaces and the coal truck backed up to the basement window, coal scattering in snow and the wooden chute was put down. The men seemed to Henry, with their merry foul language, like good souls from a netherworld of whistling darkness, their faces soot-black with pink showing in the wrinkles and the brimless bagged cap they used for carrying coal on their backs.

He was fifteen and wore grey flannels and a blue blazer with a crest on the breast pocket that said *Bonitatem, Disciplinam et Scientiam*. Every morning at 8:20 he took the subway and bus uptown to a private Catholic boys' school. His briefcase and overcoat seemed too big and he looked like a small, frail businessman. At school he kept to himself. His locker had been hammered with rotten fruit. He was occasionally pushed around and mimicked. At lunch, he'd had to choose a table where he'd be left alone, usually with an electronics whiz known as Mr. Resistor, a kid who was obsessed with Lenin, and another who spoke almost no English. As soon as he could, he went home. It was 1962 and there were only six channels on television so he watched just about anything. He would spend the rest of the evening in his room on his homework which he was terrified of not finishing. It was halfway down the hall and had a tall window onto an alley. There, nothing impinged. The walls were his walls.

One morning in February, as he was on his way to the subway, he passed two girls. They were black. He thought they lived just up the block in a beat-up brick apartment house with a two-storey portico, nearly unpainted pillars, and rusting cornice mouldings bent against the sky. The taller girl asked, "Hey you, you got the time?" She spoke as if she knew him, chewing gum and suddenly bursting out laughing. He looked at his watch and told her the time and went on. She was the better dressed and had lipstick and dangling gold earrings and was always talking and looking around She seemed to be in her late teens. The shorter girl, a little older, seemed serious and kept more to herself.

He was failing science, math and geography. Science was his worst subject. Father Martin had asked the class to memorize a hundred and fifty-two molecular structures. And just the day before, he had asked Henry to draw ammonia and five related structures on the board. Henry tried but could not get beyond ammonia itself. A kid called Wilkins whispered wrong answers to him and there was laughter. Wilkins was captain of the junior hockey team. Once, before class, he had kicked Henry's books across the floor and when Henry scrambled to get them, Wilkins kicked them all over the room until they were broken and torn to pieces. Henry thought, Even if he decides to beat me up, I won't run because he can't touch who I am, the person I am when I'm by myself.

About a week later, he tried to memorize all the ammonia and gave up. Then his mother sent him down to the drugstore at the corner and he saw the younger black girl again, the taller one. She was at the bus stop, stamping against the cold. She wore a long fake mink coat with the collar turned up around her ears and through it a glint of rhinestone. She grinned and said "Hi," loud again. Her teeth were chattering. It seemed for a moment that she was about to take his hands in hers and press them until they were warm. He was moving toward the door of the store when she said, "So, how's it goin'?" She was chewing gum.

He turned and said, "I'm okay."

"Just okay, huh," she said.

"Yeah," he said, holding the door.

"You know any good clubs around?"

"Clubs?

"Nightclubs," she said. "I guess you don't go, huh. Not yet anyway."

"I don't really know about that."

"This city is bad – bad for clubs," she said. "Only one good club in town, the Bluebird, you know that one? On Bathurst.

But we're gettin' a little sick of that one. Not like in Detroit. The clubs there the best."

He wanted to say something, if only to be in the same world for a moment, but all he could say was, "I just read books – I read history generally."

"Yeah?"

"I don't really go out that much."

"You live in that big house on the corner."

"Yeah, with my parents," he said.

"That's some fine property," she said.

"We rent the ground-floor apartment."

"We live up the street, the house with them white pillars."

"Right."

The bus was behind a line of traffic at the light. She glanced at it. "You should come to the Bluebird sometime," she said. "Cut loose a little bit. I can get you in. Forget about your age. I know them. Give you a great time."

"Right," he said. She was crazy. The bus pulled up.

"Next time I see you I'll tell you when." She laughed and disappeared.

He failed science and math. He tried to make friends but he was shy and formal. He had a brother but his brother was at school in Europe. He began to sense something dark and devouring but was unable to say what it was because he couldn't distinctly separate it from everything else. Sometimes on the subway home he struggled not to think about this darkness but even then it was somehow present. Over him or just behind him. Sometimes at night he imagined what it might be like to not waken; it would be weightless floating, like sleep. There'd no longer be the days that went on and on.

By March a thaw had begun and everywhere the eaves rained water steadily and the trees were black and wet against the sky and then it would freeze again. He had begun to look at books his father had on the French Revolution. The books seemed to make another world, a world he would get lost in for long periods. On a Saturday, the coal truck was pulling away from next door and the men were folding the sacks. Rain had begun and Henry was breaking ice out of the gutter when the girl he had met at the bus stop passed down the other side of the street. She rocked back with a laugh as if they had some running joke and this time he laughed, then she said something that was drowned out by the coal truck and when it drove off she called, "So, you goin' to the Bluebird?"

"The what?"

"I told you we could get you in?" She spoke as if he already knew it.

"Oh, right," he said. The only club he had heard of was the Towne because he'd seen it in the newspapers, the first time he'd ever learned of gangsters in the city, gangsters and gamblers running the clubs and causing trouble. A gambler had almost been beaten to death in the Towne.

She paused and said, but without mocking, "You aren't scared, are you?"

"No," he said. He didn't want to be scared. "Yeah, I was thinking. I might," he said. They were shouting over the rain.

"Friday," she said.

"I don't know," he said.

"If you're comin', come by the house about nine," she shouted. "We'll be ready then. Just dress to go out," she said. "We'll be comin' back here so you come back with us. Your folks won't mind? Nobody's gonna give you liquor or nothing." She turned to go then turned back. "What's your name?"

"Henry," he said.

"I'm Maxine."

That night at midnight Maxine threw a piece of ham with maple syrup into a frying pan. Her sister, Marsha, sat in a housecoat painting her nails and said, "What the fuck you think you doing? He's underage. He got parents. And he's white. And he lives on this street. You crazy?"

"This ain't Detroit, this is Toron-to. Nobody won't even notice it one time. Anyway, Gus do like I tell him."

"Maxine? He's a kid."

"He looks like he ain't got nothing to do. He's probably never been nowhere. Probably never even has a good time." Except, she thought, this kid, the way he was, like he'd never change for nobody. This faraway look that he had that felt like forever.

"I hope to hell you'd never cross that line. He's not even sixteen."

"I ain't doing nothin' except what I said I'd do."

"I sure as hell hope not."

Maxine turned on her sister. "What you thinkin' in your filthy mind, girl? Can't you just picture a kid like that watchin' the Hurricanes? He'd be knocked down."

Marsha put the cap back on the nail polish bottle. She had never understood her sister. Her sister caused trouble for fun, for high spirits. Marsha had had the same man for two years now and Maxine had never had one for more than two months and was always trying to prove to Marsha that Marsha's life was dull, that being that long with somebody was a slow death. Maxine always had to prove that she could do anything and survive it. Even their mother had said she was crazy. And she was. The Bluebird was the only big black club in Toronto in 1962 and for those who went there that was the world. But after a silence they burst out laughing and she laughed a high peel and Marsha laughed now with her.

"Now girl," Marsha said, "just mind your manners."

The next day in school Father Procopio perused the class gravely until the tittering and talking fell to uneasy quiet. He waited almost five minutes until everyone was still. The priest looked down, put his hands behind his back and began to stroll. On Friday he had asked them to write two hundred words on the meaning of life. He paused. The average mark had been a disappointing 6.1. But that wasn't the worst part. The problem was that a student had written an abomination. He had written that God had made the world as his plaything, a concentration camp, so He could watch us all suffer. The implications were serious and the student had been suspended. Now perhaps they did not know what Gnosticism was. The Gnostics believed in a God who didn't care – who allowed people to be ruled by the devil. The believers in a Gnostic god were bound for hell. A guileless and earnest student named Spiegler, who wore heavy horn-rims, had jet-black hair and acne, asked why God allowed all the suffering in the world anyway. Father Procopio said such a question wasn't on the curriculum, opened a book, licked his finger, turned a page and began the day's lesson.

On Friday he didn't change out of his school blazer and tie and flannels. He looked at one of the books on the French Revolution in the study and he thought about not going to the club. But not going meant everything would be the same. He watched *Gunsmoke*, wondering if maybe he just went out the door without saying anything his mother would assume he had gone over to visit the kids of family friends. At nine-thirty he put on his coat and went out.

The entrance to his parents' place was scuffed black and white marble. It had no smell except for the dead leaves that had blown in and crumbled in the fall and it was always chilly. Up the street, the entrance to Maxine and Marsha's place greeted him with a blast of heat as soon as he went in. It smelled of cooking. He didn't want to stay there long. He heard children and radios above, and someone yelling. He knocked lightly. Marsha opened the door.

"Yeah, come in," she said. She seemed irritated. There was a loud radio playing. He closed the door. Marsha said, "Come on, nobody told you to stand there. Excuse this mess. It's not mine, it's all hers." He wasn't sure if she was Maxine's sister, she seemed a little heavier than he remembered.

As he came into the kitchen Maxine lit a cigarette, shaking the match and tossing it, streaming a furl of smoke into the sink, balancing on one foot and closing one eye, the cigarette dangling from her lips, saying, "Don't believe her, she's lyin', it's her mess."

"Bitch," Marsha said, and they burst out laughing. Maxine wore a skinny red satin dress that hugged her thighs and her hair was up in assured grandeur and she said, "Marsha, this is Henry. This is my sister Marsha."

"You gotta be careful with her," Marsha said and Maxine smacked her arm with the back of her hand.

"Go get ready," said Maxine. She told Henry to sit down and he was offered macaroni and pop and cookies but he refused, saying repeatedly, "No thanks, it's okay." Maxine was talking on the telephone now. The kitchen too was old and high ceilinged. It was in old farmhouse cream colour, with the linoleum worn to black cracks. Through the back window he could see lumber and junk in the wet darkness of the yard. Maxine glanced at him as she talked. He hoped he would not be asked any questions or asked to dance.

At the Bluebird, standing by the coat check and velvet rope barrier, Maxine spoke with Gus, a small, old black man in a tuxedo. She talked nonstop while Gus could only get two words in. It was clear that it was about him, about Henry, and Marsha was looking dimly at her sister, almost pursing her lips, but she leaned to Henry and said, "That's Gus, don't worry about nothing." They waited and Gus turned and talked to another man and the man looked at Henry, then at Maxine who said impatiently, "Come on," and took Henry by the hand and yanked him through. Marsha said to him, "Gus let you in. Just don't do nothing' and don't pay no attention to Maxine. She'll say anything."

At the top of red-carpeted stairs a burst of sapphire light and exploding chords of horns shook his chest. The place was packed, he felt an overwhelming closeness and intimacy and a secret dark freedom. They went to a wall table and sat down. Maxine asked what he wanted and he said Coke. The band loomed over him, the lights on their faces like rainy neon – streaming in perspiration, jackets dancing with sequin fire. His eyes got used to the light and he saw that there were stucco arches and potted palms. A man, his face almost absent in the darkness above a white dinner jacket, took Maxine to dance. Marsha leaned forward.

"That's her man," she said.

"Her what?"

"Her boyfriend," Marsha said in his ear.

"Oh," he said. The men all wore pointed shoes with a shine that flashed. He felt conscious of the crest on his jacket and the scuffed oxfords. The drinks came round and he took a half sip and the taste was harsh but he swallowed it. He asked what it was.

Maxine laughed, "You've got ours. Rum and Coke. They made a mistake."

Marsha screamed but Henry saw she was laughing too, rising toward a big light-skinned man in a navy double-breasted suit. Maxine rolled her eyes and said something he could not hear, something about Marsha's man being a jerk. Henry shifted and sat closer beside her. He had only been to one dance, at his high school where they all seemed angular and jiggling. But here they all seemed to move without effort though they seemed to be strangers. While Marsha danced, her cheek lay on the back of her hand, which was flat on the man's arm and she seemed so submissive after the tough way she had been with her sister. Maxine pointed to Henry's drink and said, "Go on. There's hardly no rum in it. You don't want it?" Her bluntness made him awkward.

Right then he wanted to be in his room sitting up in bed with the book about Danton he had from the library. He had got to the meeting between Robespierre and Danton in a restaurant and wondered when Robespierre would turn against his old friend and then he had the odd thought that it was all one with this room; the splendour of the clothes in those days and of this club, and the peculiar, impractical and senseless splendour of Maxine who now spoke into his ear, her breath as cool as if it had come over snow. He felt the light pressure on his sleeve of her slender fingers, her nails were on his jacket, and he thought of how the nap was gone from his jacket and how it was probably dirty from school, and for some reason that made her touch feel like kindness. The gold pendant leaf of her earring turned and caught the light and swung. She rested her right hand flat against the side of her thigh and drank with her left, her knuckles touched his leg lightly. He wondered if black skin had an odour, as someone had said at school. They were silent for a while and then she said, "You wanna learn to dance?"

Afraid, he did not want to answer.

"There's an easy number coming up. You can fake it."

He laughed and sipped the rum and Coke and said, "I don't think so. I'm pretty bad."

Marsha and the big man came back to a long, elegiac blast of horns. He could hear them in a short silence saying something about Cleveland and then: "Them women like furnaces burning in the night, like hellfire," and a fat man with gold rings extended his hand to Maxine who got up and joined him on the dance floor and Henry felt momentary surprise and confusion and jealousy. Marsha sat at the end of the wall seat now. She mopped sweat off her brow with a napkin. Something dissolved in him. He wished there were more of the rum and Coke – the last of it now soaking the ice that twinkled ultramarine in the dark. He saw Marsha watching the dance floor intently. He would never tell anyone about this. He would go on living and secretly he would always have this, something only these girls could have given him, that did not seem part of this life.

Back from her dance, Maxine sat down and lit a cigarette. The bandleader did a solo and there were whoops and cheers. Henry felt her power again in the dark, a dim hot silhouette beside him, something inexpressible that he could not understand except its vaguely having the power of a woman and he shifted with the feeling of excitement growing in his groin.

They all stood up to go. He tried to contribute some money but she said next time and he insisted because there probably couldn't be a next time. Outside there was fog and he walked a little ahead because the girls were drunk, laughing and talking on top of each other, and then kept stopping and bending over hurting with laughter and he turned and watched them. Then they all went on, the girls chattering and laughing and letting out screams, and between it all Maxine saying, "The world is shit down here and God knows it and so when you get a better job or get a man or get some lovin', that's God givin' it to you because He knows He can't give you nothing else 'cause he made a big mistake and went and lost everybody," and Marsha whooped.

He went on ahead and when he got home it was about one o'clock. He felt sophisticated and sort of drunk. In the dark his mother stood, short and ghostly in the door of the bedroom, and said, "I've been beside myself."

"It's okay, I had a long walk," he said.

He tried to sound sincere as he apologized. She looked at him, maintaining a tormenting silence. He looked down. She started again: "It didn't occur to you, of course, that I might not be able to sleep thinking anything might have happened to you."

"I'm very, very sorry," he said. She looked at him for a long while and then closed her bedroom door. The house seemed his in the darkness.

On Monday after school, when Henry got out of the subway, he went a distance west to a record store. He did not know what to ask for but looked until he found a record with six black musicians on it. The music was called "soul" and he bought it. Over the next few days he had thought he might see the girls on the street again but he didn't and somehow it seemed as if they had never been, as if it had never happened. He kept the record in his room and looked at it every day wondering what they would do if somehow he could give it to them.

It had been raining Saturday afternoon and as Marsha opened the door, sleet and hail began to rattle down everywhere – as if winter were moving backwards. She was in her housecoat and she turned, leaving the door open and went ahead of him down the hall, and so he stepped in. She shouted that Maxine was out but she was coming back and there was some stew on the stove if he wanted some. She was just watching TV and he could sit down in the living room. He sat carefully on the corner of the dark red sofa and put the record down on a side table. *Abbott and Costello* was on television, and Marsha sat down, picked up her cigarette and watched the TV. She barely acknowledged his presence and only when he found himself listening for the door did he realize maybe he had really come to see Maxine and that somehow Marsha knew he had. And then the tap of a footstep and the door opening in the entrance. And then the apartment door.

"It is shit out there," she said. Under her coat she had on grey check pedal-pushers and a white cashmere sweater. She dropped a bag of groceries in the hall and without pause wiggled her fingers at him and said "Hi" as if she had known he would be there. She had changed her hair and he suddenly missed the way it had been before. He would never see that again. She disappeared and he listened as she unbuttoned her coat in the hall and it seemed to take forever before she came back in. She plumped herself down on the other end of the sofa. She lit a cigarette and then said, "So, what's happenin' with you?" Marsha impassively watched Abbott hand a pie to Costello. Maxine passed her cigarettes around and then stopped and said, "You don't smoke?"

"No," he said.

They were silent, then Marsha got up and left the room.

Maxine picked up the *TV Guide* and leafed through. It didn't seem to matter that he was there. Maxine looked at her watch and said she had to wash her hair because they had to go and see her aunt later. Henry said he had to be going soon anyway. He sat up and handed her the record. She looked at it, dragging on the cigarette and said, "I never heard of them," and turned it over and looked at it and gently put it down. "Thanks."

They gazed at *Abbott and Costello.* Marsha, dressed in her coat, went out the front door.

Maxine said, "So what you been up to?"

"Oh, not much," he said too loudly and sitting up straight. "I've been reading this book."

She was examining a crack in her nail, and said, "Yeah? What's it about?"

"About this guy in the..." He didn't know how to proceed. "...in the French Revolution, called Danton..." She frowned slightly. "He was killed. In France in 1794. In three months alone they killed four thousand people in the city of Paris."

"Who did?"

"The government," he said. "The Jacobins. They killed this Danton guy too."

"Who were they?"

"A political party."

He told her about the guillotine and the fast trials. He tried to make it sound interesting. She listened, glancing at the TV as she smoked. He didn't know whether to stay or not, whether she didn't know how to ask him to leave or maybe she just had nothing better to do. He kept waiting for her to get up but she just sat there. It had gotten darker. The street lights came on.

"So, what did you think of the club?"

He said he liked the music. He said that sometimes he heard music like it when he listened to the radio late at night.

He asked her what she thought of the club and she said she was getting tired of it. It was the best and the worst. The best and the worst people. He asked her what she meant and she looked at the ember of her cigarette and said, "I don't know... You love it, you get sick of it, you don't go for a while and then it all comes back to you and you fall in love with it again." He had an image of light and fire in darkness like the furnaces of a city at night. "It's like it's always there. It's all there is."

Looking for a match she got up suddenly and said offhand, "Everybody needs love," and she picked up matches and lit another cigarette. He had never heard anyone speak about love like that as if it were simple like food or water. As if it were anything except something needed for marriage or for children, or some fragile gift from God or something dangerous, complex and delicate that had to be nurtured in relationships or something sacred. She eased herself back down. He saw how slim her legs were and how tight her backside. He wondered whom she loved. For a while they didn't speak and then she said, "Men, they act like they don't need love but they need it, but they say they don't, they treat themselves like they don't and they treat you like you don't neither, like it's just some win-or-lose game and that starts everybody else playin' games. That's one thing you gotta watch if you ever go there," she said. He wondered if she meant they would never go there together. If he would not see her again. They fell into silence. Outside it had turned to wet snow again and it fell heavy and straight in the street lights. At length she said, "Excuse me, there's just somebody really makin' me mad."

"You love this person?" he said.

"I don't love nobody," she said.

He asked her where she was from. She was from Detroit. Her mother had run into problems and she'd sent her and Marsha to stay in Toronto with their aunt who had married a Trinidadian grocer, west off Bathurst Street, and they had lived back and forth ever since. This time the aunt and her husband had taken a short trip to Trinidad and the girls were alone. Henry asked which she liked better, Detroit or Toronto.

"Here you don't get killed, there you don't get bored."

He said, "You've got to know this city." But then he realized that the things he liked were places you walked to, views, things that seemed old, things he could not put into words. They were silent again. She got up and turned the TV volume down to the image alone, flicked through the channels, past the CBLT news and left it silent on *The Donna Reed Show* and came back and turned, falling backward against the back of the sofa so that her right calf landed up against his arm, her cigarette bobbing in the dark. He could hear the radio from the kitchen, the remote murmur of a crescendo of horns, with tearful heaven-bound grandeur and something about a river and salvation. It was almost dark now and there was only the paleness from the street lights and the TV. On the floor above, someone was vacuuming.

"You're nice," she said.

He did not know what to say.

"You should fix yourself up, fix your shirt." She poked his knee for emphasis. "Or the little man is going to get you," and smiling she walked her fingers up his thigh and poked her nail through the gap in his shirt. He flinched and laughed. He heard the whisper of her clothes before he realized she was close and looking directly at him. He put a hand lightly and haltingly on her shoulder and she bent her head a little and closed her eyes and from her care and her slowness he could tell that it was obvious to her he had never done this. He kissed her carefully and his pale hands were behind her shoulders, trembling a little, and he felt that her mouth was open and so he opened his mouth, too. She said "Mmm" as if it tasted good. Then, "I think you're the first man I ever kissed that didn't never smoke." No one had ever called him a man.

There wasn't the dark violent mystery or the earthenness he had expected but a very slight tartness, perhaps of perspiration, her flesh cool everywhere on the surface, warm underneath and the same perfume, lighter now. An uncomplicated giving, a slow and insensate warmth and darkness without time or remembering. And yet this is what he would remember long after, long after the furnaces and the coal men were gone, how when she had swung to the side and sat up, the briefest glimmer in darkness of her pale labia, her breasts in brief and sudden profile in a penumbra of light; and as she stood and turned, the wicked explosion of her pubic hair in the halo of the street lamp seen and gone.

Over the next weeks, terrific winds came and left bits of branches in the road. He did not see her in the street. He phoned and Marsha took a message. Once, he knocked. The window was black and you could not see in and he wondered if they had moved. In class, he imagined her going by in the Bathurst Street bus, going by like a ghost. He wondered how and why he had known them, why the world was so masked and wordless.

He got up every day and took the subway to school. In math class, the wallet his father had brought him from India was taken and passed up and down the rows as the boys tore it slowly to pieces, and when the bell rang the destroyed pieces were formally handed back to him in a heap. He cared even less now because he had something that felt as exclusive as it was inviolable, in fact untouchable, and which made stronger the part of himself that was content to be alone anyway. It was now warm enough to eat his lunch outside and he sat in a place where he had sat before and which he regarded as his own, a solitude in which there was another presence. At dusk he passed the house with the unpainted columns, wondering if the last of the icicles that hung from the tin cornice had been there since that evening, the one he was to go on recalling. In the empty street at night the sisters fell to him like angels of light at night, she herself like white fire.

He remembered that in his childhood, when he couldn't sleep, he had sometimes turned on a scratched wooden radio that no one used, its dial an oval of glowing parchment. Inside, you could see the elastic cord for the dial bar coated in dust. On clear cold nights on low volume, remote and elegiac behind static, there had been that music, intoxicating and violent, fecund and controlled and associated with darkness and winter and it came over the roofs and through the wall; from the west through green stars high in the night, something about Detroit, at least the station was Detroit. Then, they had only been voices. He did not know until now that they had been black.

THE CHANGE

At midnight, she had a plane for Heathrow and she wouldn't be coming back. It was final. More final than the family knew. What did it matter? She was sixty-three. All she needed was good reading. The Book Store in Yorkville had been a godsend. They did orders for her, Sheila Last. They knew her: well dressed, short and assertive with faded red hair. She wore dark prescription glasses interchangeably with her other glasses, often without regard to the light. She picked up Beckett's *Watt* to re-read in case of a layover. Her husband, Stuart, had never understood Beckett. Most people didn't. She got the *New Statesman* and the *Spectator*. Those should get her through the flight with a stinger or two. She would bring her father's edition of *Bleak House*. A Sumerian burial.

Avenue Road was invisible for the fog. She wouldn't have a drink until she was on the plane. She wanted no goodbyes; she just wanted to be gone. She crossed Avenue Road. You couldn't see Queen's Park. Fog evoked her father and he faded and she went into the lounge in the Park Plaza and had a salad and read the *Spectator*. A daiquiri wouldn't hurt. But she'd forego a double. She had the daiquiri and read an item about Mrs. Bhutto and Pakistan and an amusing piece on the

Rolling Stones. The Rolling Stones were true originals. The daiquiri would do her until the flight. The only thing that bothered her was the actual moment of departure that evening; she wasn't interested in anyone's final words.

She went home along Lowther Avenue. Her life had somehow been lived along Lowther, age-old and shrouded with towering trees and old houses, you sort of forgot it. Like some primordial axis but underground. The old literary crowd had all lived around there. She had brought internationally renowned stars to her marriage in the great age of the war years. Many were famous now. Like the critic, Preston Ewart. She had been at their centre, herself a rising star. She wondered if they even thought of her now. Failure opened in the road, a quake, a black chasm and then it was only asphalt. She still had her novel. All in her head. She had dropped it off with Preston around '49, he hadn't responded, a tactful silence, she'd asked for it back and she'd gone up and taken it back and that was that. Then she had mislaid it. Perhaps Stuart had filed it somewhere. Anyhow, she had let it wait.

The intersection of Lowther and St. George Street appeared; visible in the fog was the space of road where her mother had been killed in a blizzard. A drunken driver, 1947. As of midnight that too would be gone. Of course the family would write and everything went blank, the stern of a Viking ship disappearing in mist. She lit a cigarette.

At Spadina the fog was darker. Or the day. She'd never needed a watch. On the corner, the shadow of the ornate brick low-rise where she and her sister Carol had grown up, its narrow balustrades stark in the greyness, unreal. Dante. "Unreal city." They had been devout Catholics. The high, white curved collar and tie of her father, the pince-nez on his lapel, reddish hair parted in the middle, square Irish face, thin mouth about to smile. She'd been four and there'd been fog and she'd been afraid and he'd taken her out on the balustrade and told her to pass her hand through it to show it meant no harm. He'd held her on his lap and read her *The Arabian Nights* and *Don Quixote*. Some or someone had said she and Daddy were too close, perhaps her sister Carol. She laughed. Here Lowther too ended.

She crossed two streets and went up to the house. She knew as soon as she opened the door that no one was in. Always such a relief to have the house to herself. She stood in the dining room and lit a cigarette. If the house had always been this quiet, she could have recomposed her novel out of her head. There was still time but you had to be completely alone and there'd been too many distractions. It would be easy to have a drink now but she wouldn't. Not until the plane. She would miss the house. It was a fine house. She had chosen it twenty-five years before. She had decided to look after the house instead of working. For some reason Carol, who still lived with them, kept taking over. Carol always seemed to think everything was on the verge of collapse. Sheila went upstairs. Her suitcase was open on the bed, half packed, her mink coat laid out beside it. She placed the *Spectator* and the Beckett in the carry-on bag and went across to the library and read the *New Statesman*.

Carol came in and said, "Hello, lovey," and handed her the *Globe and Mail*. Carol still wore round glasses from the 'forties. There was something ascetic about her. She could have been a nun. She taught the Victorian Novel at the university. "My, this fog," she said, lighting a cigarette. "So little snow this year. It's like London already." They talked about fog and Wilde and Dickens. Carol told Sheila she had added some extra items to the suitcase and said she'd miss her and that she'd write every day. They agreed they'd miss the house.

There was no turning back. Once Sheila moved to England on a monthly allowance from Stuart, Stuart would sell the house. Carol had accepted a position teaching on loan to Chicago. Stuart was considering an old cottage on Georgian Bay and an apartment in the Tuscan mansion whose first floor was occupied by his office, Darnton, Last, Publicists. It had been Sheila's choice to take a hotel in London: the theatre, restaurants, music and galleries in Toronto were all second-rate.

Her biggest concern, she now said to Carol, "is my dear son, Henry." He was only twenty-five and living alone in some appalling little room a few streets over. Carol said they'd all keep in touch. Henry was the one person on earth, Sheila told herself, she truly loved. Yet he seemed indifferent to her, almost callous. Supposedly he was coming tonight.

Carol asked her if she was hungry. Sheila told Carol not to get up, she'd get herself something. She picked up the newspaper and went down to the dining room and took a full bottle of vermouth out of the sideboard. She poured a glass, started it slowly and finished it quickly. She gazed at the mist in the garden. Her father again. No one had ever really known Daddy but her. His Panama hat, the waterfront, the island, the

Exhibition fair grounds. He'd taken her everywhere, just the two of them. On the Ferris wheel. She was about to put the bottle back but no one would be looking for the liquor, not tonight, and she went to the basement stairs and placed the vermouth among some empty bottles by the steps.

She went back up to the library. Carol examined her quickly, looked back to her book. Sheila picked up the newspaper, lit another cigarette. The door closed downstairs. Stuart came up. In a suit, vest and tie, exasperated, as though he'd come home from work, though it was a holiday and he'd come from an office party. He said he was glad it was over. He was heavyset, precise, dutiful, stamped his heel as he spoke. Sheila had once admired his elegance, his erudition, his sense of the ridiculous, but he was not the man he had once been; he was balding and rather senatorial now and either he ignored her or looked on her with suspicion. She couldn't tell how he felt about this evening or about anything really. He turned to her with that patient formality and said, "They called at the office. Your flight is delayed by the weather. It's one in the morning. I've arranged for a car." He put on his reading glasses and examined a list from his pocket.

"Where is my love, Henry?" Sheila demanded. Carol and Stuart said he was on his way. He was the one she would truly miss. Stuart reflected aloud, "I wonder what they're all doing for New Year's." They had cancelled their New Year's party a week before Christmas. Carol asked Sheila if she had done all the calls. "Believe you me, every last one," Sheila said. "I wouldn't have wanted a party this year anyway. I'm tired of the whole crew." She got up and said she was going to have a lie-down.

She went into the hall. You couldn't see the bedroom door from the library. She closed the door loudly enough to be heard and went quietly downstairs and through the kitchen to the basement stairs where she found the vermouth. She had forgotten the glass. She had a glass in the basement where a little light from the street threw long shadows from the barred windows. In the corner was a trunk, the armoire from Spadina, and Daddy's hat stand. She put down the bottle, sat on the trunk and found the glass. She spat and wiped it out with a handkerchief and filled it.

The tone used about Sheila when she wasn't there was hushed, respectful, exasperated, the way doctors and relatives speak of a difficult patient. Carol said, "She's tight." She and Stuart tried to figure out how long she'd been drinking and how much. Carol had seen and smelled the glass in the kitchen. Stuart swore under his breath. Carol reassured him that Sheila really did want to go. He said he certainly hoped so: he had the real estate agent coming tomorrow. "I think you could have waited a day or two," Carol said and cut herself off: "Okay, I'll shut up," and he said, "I spared her the sign on the front lawn."

In the silence of the basement, the past, the truth, became satisfyingly clear. Of course Stuart was a stoic; he had hidden his feelings about the old group: the university poets and critics, Ewart, McAlastair and the rest had regarded him as an outsider from New Brunswick, a successful publicist of mainstream authors. Not one of the fold. Too much money, too nimble, too well dressed. As for her, she had spoken her mind when it was dangerous, even self-destructive for a woman to do so. Of course there had been her indiscretions, so she had been told. But it was the silence, the courteous twenty-five year silence that had been unbearable. Stuart claimed she had alienated them. But it was Stuart who'd been the barrier between her and her friends.

In the library, Stuart glanced toward the bedroom: "Now we have to deal with her waking up. And you know what that's like." His sister-in-law reminded him that he had loved her and probably still did and he said, "Carol, don't be ridiculous," with that vicious, withering darkness of people who have repressed too much for too long. Carol lit a cigarette. He poured himself a scotch from the desk. Carol looked at him and said, "Do you think you should? In front of her?" and he said, "What on earth difference is it going to make now? If she goes on the plane drunk, she goes on the plane drunk."

The street light through the bars of the basement window became the late sun setting through the columns of the Princes' Gates at the Exhibition, 1927 or so, and her father, well read, too trusting, failed at business, retired early in poor health. Above all, gentle. He had told her to be determined like a man, never to care what anyone thought, had told her she would experience the change that occurred in great artists during inspiration, a crisis. He'd told her she would do great things. As if he feared the world were falling apart and she was soon to take charge. The Ferris wheel, sailing like love, so close. Years later he was dead and she and her mother had had a fight. Her mother had gone out and Sheila had assumed she'd return during the blizzard but her mother hadn't come back. The drunk driver had got off because he was from a rich family. Daddy would have dealt with the drunk driver but Daddy was dead.

They were Catholic and she had been left with the death unreconciled and the unreconciled quarrel that had preceded it and it felt it like a blot, like a stain.

Upstairs, Henry had come in, wild and violent-eyed as he poured a scotch, unkempt, hair awry, sideburns, wearing a tie. Carol said, "Thank you for putting on a tie for your mother." Henry said, "As long as I don't have to be alone with her." His father said, "She is a very unhappy woman. I think we owe her a little peace. At least until the plane." Henry said, "Who owes who peace?" Henry was trying to be a poet. His father had offered to rent him a proper space but Henry insisted on a shabby rented room.

In the basement, the vermouth brought her to the high, rounded white collar carrying her, flying, on the island ferry, the trees hot and delicious in summer, in his arms on the Ferris wheel, candy floss, being carried high through grownup guests in the yellow drawing room on Spadina at New Year's, the two of them, anthropos, hermaphrodite, centaur, the Greeks would have understood, Preston Ewart would have understood. Yet despite his *Criticism: Lines of Descent and Evolution*, he had failed so thoroughly to understand Beckett. Otherwise he had been the only person she could really talk to. Daddy had pretended to look into a crystal ball and said she would hold court in hotel rooms across Europe like the expatriates, Joyce, Eliot, Pound. Daddy had said, "The son I never had, I am lonely, your mother has lost interest." Daddy and I were together, the two of us, on a prow out of the fog. And then Henry, the last loved.

She appeared in the library holding on to the doorway. Carol half rose: "Dear, you have your dark glasses on. You're going to fall." Stuart mouthed loudly to Carol, "She's got to be on the plane tonight." Sheila came in slowly, surveying the room and said, "Have the guests gone? Or have they not arrived?" Everyone was silent. She turned carefully and stared at Henry for a long time. "There is the boy I love," she said. Henry said, "Hello there." Sheila asked Carol if she'd got the hors d'oeuvres, the canapés. Carol cleared her throat and said loudly, "You have a flight for London, dear." Sheila said, "What flight to London?" Henry said, "The Flying Dutchman," and his mother laughed and said, "Well! Quite right!" and she remembered her parents' ditty and said, "Good morning, Mrs. Harding, is that our kitting in your garding and all the way to London? What a long way from home!" Stuart turned to her and said something about the weather, the fog, a second flight delay and her having to be at the airport at one-thirty in the morning for a two-thirty flight. "Well, joke over," she said, "I presume we're having New Year's." Gently, they told her she'd agreed to the whole thing as late as this morning, that it had been her idea to begin with: London and a room at the Basil Street Hotel. The same old fraud, she thought. Carol was trying to look sympathetic. Again, Stuart exhumed the old fiction of her being drunk. Carol pleaded to Sheila that she had packed her own bags and put the magazines in herself, and Sheila turned and said to Carol, *"Et tu, Brute?"* Carol asked her to go and look at the bags and Sheila said, "So it was you who did that. Well. I see. What have I got? An hour? Then, what? Instead of the sanatorium, the old way. Exile. Who was it? Ovid? Ovid sent into exile because he knew too much!" Henry called out, "How about Saint Helena!" Carol said, "Henry, stop!" Sheila said to Henry, "Well, old boy, you don't love me. You are not telling me anything new."

She'd always known that they talked about her behind her back as if she were insane. Then had come their discreet plans to edge her out. "I know you all don't want me here," she said, and her son said, "How about this? If you don't go, we'll go." Carol and Stuart made a show of reprimanding him. Their concern again, it was such a charade. She thought: They are actually united. She was under attack; it was time to speak from the docket and she said, "I know perfectly well that I'm being sent away because I know too much," and Carol shouted, "Sheila, don't start!" but Sheila shouted over her: "I know that my son will never even make it as a second-rate poet. Much as I love him." And they were all interrupting, trying to stop her and she had to shout over them. "And that my husband became an agent because he couldn't write and became a publicist because he couldn't become an agent. And my sister who teaches, what is it? The bluffer's guide to *The Mill on the Floss!*" She half collapsed on a chair near the door. Her novel was alive, it burned brightly somewhere among Daddy's things, or perhaps in the safes of Random House in New York. Anyhow, she had it in her head. It would go wherever she went, and Henry shouted, "Hey, Mother, come on, you love Ferris wheels! There are Ferris wheels in England! You can knock back a few Camparis and ride the Ferris wheel doing double crostics in the *Spectator!*" She raged and ordered everyone out of the room and then became drowsy, the stern of a ship going away in mist. The room was empty. Daddy would be home soon. He had always had to work late on New Year's

Eve, reporting his sales for December. Where was her drink? She looked for the bottle and glasses. They had gone.

When they had come downstairs it was dark, the only light from the fog and street light. They had brought down the whisky along with her suitcases. Carol had turned on a lamp. The living room was a parchment yellow. Carol had her knitting. She said quietly, "Stuart, why don't we just let her stay?" and he whispered, "And deal with this again on Wednesday? And the following Tuesday? Take the house off the market and deal with it every week or ten days? Forever? Carol, I avoid coming home!" They had all, in one way or another, become afraid of her.

Above, in the library, Sheila stood up slowly. It had been a bum party, whosever place this was. She went into the bedroom in the dark. Her coat was the last one on the bed.

She came downstairs. Henry whispered, "She's got her coat on." Stuart said aloud, "There you are!" She looked around, disoriented, stared at her bags, looked up and said, "Well. I am going. And I'll tell you why." She turned to Stuart. "Quite apart from everything I've become aware of—" He tried to speak but she cut him off: "You told Preston Ewart that the novel wasn't— you spoke against it. You went and got it back, so he never read it. And I haven't seen it since." Stuart was mouthing his usual denial. Genet had had his work confiscated in prison and had rewritten it out of his head. She would have to do the same, in exile. Someone said something sarcastic, the room was yellow, she'd had it done like Mother and Daddy's on Spadina back in '47 when Preston was the man she should have married but Stuart had put an end to it with the stories of her so-called madness and drinking. Apparently, she had said it aloud because Stuart replied, "Well, perhaps you should have married Preston," and she said, "In marrying me, you won a Pyrrhic victory against your betters, and now that you have failed the marriage you are sending me away." She looked at her son. He shone despite his boorishness, the line of Daddy, perhaps he would succeed where she had failed, been failed, foiled, if he could write something even remotely approaching Larkin, and she said to him, "And why you? The only one I truly love. Why have you gone along with this?" He said, "I moved out of here a long time ago, perhaps you didn't notice." Children were a bore but she'd always loved Henry, had always wanted him nearby if out of earshot. Stuart was still talking about forcing her onto a plane. New Year's Eve and here they were, trying to give her the send-off and she said, "What are you going to do about the guests?" The three were talking among themselves. Perhaps, in the final act, she ought to evoke origins, as in any well-written tragedy: "Just don't forget how you dishonoured Mother," she said to Stuart. Carol had her hands up, beseeching her to stop. "Are we not here in the apartment where it happened?" she said. Someone said it was 1975 and they were not on Spadina and she said, "Mother was killed. You were there. By a drunken driver. And Daddy was dead." Stuart shouted, "Look! Are you going to embarrass the driver? And the airline? Everyone?" She had always embarrassed people with the truth. "Daddy was dead," she said, "My mother was dishonoured. I asked you to go to the Crown prosecutor or get a lawyer to get that boy sentenced. And you did nothing! You allowed his family to get him off. Because they had influence!" He shouted,

"We didn't have the money! I had come home from the war! Everything was in disorder. I was making crumbs writing jacket flaps!" She smelled victory. He went on, "You refused to work! Carol and I didn't have the money between us!" She cut in: "The two of you bought this house!" The room swam. The floor tilted. "Three years later!" he shouted. "Anyhow," she declared, "it didn't require money. It required the exposure of corruption! Nothing a third-rate gumshoe or hack reporter couldn't do!" And Henry said to her, "Then you could have done it!" and she swung at him and he ducked and she lost her balance. Carol caught her. She pushed Carol away and turned to Stuart: "You had become head of the household. You quailed before your duty and you are responsible, if not for her death then for her unquiet grave. It's the one thing that has ruined my life."

A man appeared at the living room door, well groomed with medium-length hair, raincoat, suit and tie. They all said hello. Tom came in, leaned down and kissed his mother. She said to him, "You know that I'm being sent away." He handed her something. He'd bought her Chanel No. 5 and the *Paris Review*. For the plane. She took them from him and put them down. He said, "I can drive you to the airport." Stuart said, "We've got a car coming in an hour and a half," and she said, "No one is driving me anywhere." Tom looked around; her first-born, obedient, thoughtful, his little gifts. He had gone into advertising. She'd had him sent to first-class schools abroad for nothing. She reeled and lost her balance and Tom caught her. Henry reflected that they all liked Tom but none of them really loved him. Because all the love and worry was reserved for Henry himself, vulnerable, rude, drunk, improvident. An inchoate talent, unformed and therefore a possibility, above all his mother's last hope of being like the Joyces in Paris or in Trieste. He felt bad for Tom.

Sheila looked at Tom vaguely. "You didn't bring your wife. For New Year's! Well, I must say I'm glad. It's Eileen, isn't it?" Tom said, "Kathleen," and Sheila said, "Yes, she is quite a bore." Kathleen was pretty, educated but unsophisticated, a boob; anyhow, she hadn't that *je ne sais quoi.* Henry said, "Tom will drive you to the airport, why don't you just go with Tom. You've got your coat on. You got your bags there." She looked down. She still had her coat on. She held out her arms: "Tom. If you will." Tom paused. Everyone was silent. Tom removed her coat and laid it carefully on the sofa. She sat in the Louis XVI armchair that commanded the room. Tom remarked that she had the wrong glasses on, the dark glasses. He was being custodial. Henry told her to leave the glasses on, that she looked like something out of *Endgame.* "Hamm," she replied. "Absolutely! Ruler of a dying world!" Her son understood her. Stuart suddenly exploded and said, "What the hell are we going to do?" He's doing it again, she thought, easing her out of parties, trying to hustle her home when things had only begun. "Put on Schubert! The Trout!" she said. Tom moved toward the stereo but Henry said he would do it. He was being obliging for once, and in a moment the rattle of bones, pop music, piano, marvelous ivories of death. Henry said something about someone called Sister Morphine, the convent school. It was the Rolling Stones, excellent, and she lolled her head to the music. Her husband had his face in his hands. She called him, pointed toward the dining room and demanded a drink and Stuart said, "I am afraid not," and she ordered each of them in turn. She concentrated on Tom. Tom hovered, paralyzed.

The doorbell rang. She would refuse to go, they would have to take her by force. Henry went out and came back with Preston Ewart and his pill of a wife, Valerie, the first to arrive, they had brought a bottle. Well, the New Year's party! Preston had aged, his rimless spectacles, looking more than ever like an owl. The room was silent. Stuart was staring, confused. Carol put down her knitting and covered her mouth. Slowly, Stuart and Carol greeted, embraced them. Sheila ordered Tom to take their coats. Stuart said, "We are underequipped." Someone was apologizing for being early. The Ewarts sat on the sofa, next to her chair.

The McAlastairs arrived, Jim and Hilda. Jim's reputation was international now. More guests arrived, the old crowd. Of course. They only saw them at New Year's. Sheila told Tom to get her a drink and asked Jim McAlastair about his interview on CBC. "You talk about the electronic media being an extension of the hand that writes, you have the ear of the younger generation, do they know that you're a conservative? At heart a Milton scholar?" McAlastair gave his thin smile and spoke rapidly: "The whole conservative-liberal nexus has nothing to do with it, actually." Then she spoke and McAlastair listened. They always did. Tom had not arrived with her drink. She went into the middle hall. Her husband was talking to the sculptor Volsky and some woman in the dining room. Stuart moved toward her quickly and hissed, "What the hell did you mean by inviting these people? You have a car coming! You told me you'd cancelled New Year's. I just spoke to Carol. She said you'd called everyone and cancelled. When you were sober!" She looked at him with outrage. "You wouldn't know any of these people if it weren't for me." Stuart went away. Tom had evaded her. She found him, conveniently, with a group by the dining-room table. She told him loudly to pour her a glass of wine. She made tiny space between thumb and forefinger: "From the top!" He acquiesced.

She took her drink and went back to the corner chair in the living room and sat down, Preston and Valerie on her left, the McAlastairs and others in front. She was getting an audience. She drank and there was music and then no music and it went dark and suddenly Preston and his wife were there. They had condescended to come. They never called otherwise. "You are aware, Preston, that your entire body of work is, well, a solipsism." He frowned good-naturedly and said, "How so?" She threw her head back and said her novel would have broken his theory, "but my husband didn't want you to read it. That was why he asked for it back." There was some perplexity as the Ewarts patiently searched the air and he said, "My god, we're talking about 1949, aren't we?"

No one had put on Schubert. From somewhere next door she heard "Auld Lang Syne." There was darkness, the room was yellow, the fog was still thick out on Spadina. Where was Daddy? Preston said, "No, my dear, I did read half of it." She heard the words "absolutely brilliant," he had to be joking, she had no memory of it and then terror. He said he'd told her back then that he knew someone at Knopf in New York, the words wobbling, unreal. "Sheila, you arrived at the house and demanded it back. You took the whole thing away and that was the last anyone heard of it." He paused gently and the fear came again and then the grey-blue of the Ewarts' veranda. "Everyone knew you were brilliant. Except for you," he said. Valerie gripped his arm and looked at Sheila with dread and sympathy. He added, speaking with care, "I don't think you had the self-confidence to see it through. No one was more disappointed than I." Spadina went away and the house reasserted itself with the twenty-seven years, long and dark and shapeless. "You said you destroyed it," he added. "And I'm sorry, but the drinking hasn't helped any." She tapped her temple hard and said, "I still have it here." Even then, in the chaos, she knew that Preston knew she didn't have it anymore and everything dimmed and became fluid and there were shouts of "Happy New Year!"

The room was empty, lit only by triangles of street light in fog beyond the balustrade. Everyone must have gone. The high white collar in darkness, warm for New Year's, the balcony door was open, her father had come in, she had no idea what to do, she was supposed to do something but she wasn't old enough and the man who was the most quiet and the most forgotten, the shadowed face and finally the collar fading in light that was like moonlight, the vest, the pince-nez, he told her to go and join her mother forever and that would settle it all and he went away. Everyone had gone. There was only the hall light. Someone called her. Her coat was on. Nor had she stood up but she was standing, unsteadily. Carol came in and said, "Lovey, the car is here."

Outside, in the dark, floated the lit interior of the airport limousine.

The boys and Carol and Stuart stood in the hall. Sheila said, "I will stay. If my son Henry wants me to stay. So, Henry, my true love, you can say so. Or not."

The car moved over the face of the earth, a black speck on the lit freeway, the only motion through the city and the night. The interior of the car was deep, dark grey plush; the ride was silent, smooth, effortless. She lit a cigarette. Indeed, it was more like a ship. Behind her the lights of the city grew fainter, slowly disappeared. It was done. Or, as someone had once said, "It is finished."

ELMIRA RAWLINSON

In the first light of dawn, she passed through the gate and turned west on the road to Connemara Station. Behind her, in the east, was the entire past of Leith, where the old, disused station was, now gone forever. The land was cold and black and Venus hung on the horizon, the star Tom had told her about. He had known about that sort of thing and had said the constellations rang like bells and she could almost feel him now, walking beside her in the dark and with him came the myriad talking and yelling of the crowd, two months ago, in the dying main street of Leith. She had been gathering chamber pots in the Grand Hotel and went out to see because this time the noise didn't die down and she heard his voice above it all and after an hour of violence and blood her life up to that day ended. And now she was leaving for good except that she carried it all inside her, the great music and turbulence and grandeur, growing and alive.

Elmira Rawlinson had first seen Tom Phair in the schoolyard, the new boy standing still and alone where the boys' yard met the girls'. Even then, he had the bearing of a lord and she asked his name and looking away from her, he said with defiance, "Thomas." Only later did she notice that he was ungainly and his jacket and boots were too big and his breeches too short, the only one in hand-me-downs as if somehow he wasn't a Phair. The boys picked on him and he avoided fighting but when he had no choice he fought badly and wildly and she'd try to defend him and even kicked a boy in the privates before Tom told her to mind her own business. He lost fight after fight, in the schoolyard, at the crossroads, in lanes, in fields, on barn floors.

On school mornings, she would let her brothers go ahead and she'd wait at the gate until Tom came along, slow and ambling, and pretend to fall in beside him by accident or after school she'd walk near him and then somehow alongside but he was only polite and soon she had his name in hearts on trees and fence posts, certain that it was only a matter of time. She'd never seen her reflection because her mother allowed no mirrors in the house but she saw herself in the eyes of the older boys who ogled her and with whom she would play secret games like "Craggshaw," where they drew lots to be a "Craggshaw," evil men from a fairy tale who captured women, burned houses and killed people, and she'd run screaming until the one that got to be Craggshaw found her alone in the cloak room or behind the outhouse and they'd kiss and feel one another but she could never get Tom to play or even to come close. Instead, she thought of him day and night.

At the end of the eighth grade, when everyone went back to the farm, she cried for a week because now he'd only pass on a wagon or in Leith or walking with his brothers with axes to the bush, but also because he had somehow meant the vague hope of release from her mother and father and brothers and the unpainted house and dilapidated barns on the ridge of badly tended fields. She did not know that the whole township itself lay under a different cosmos, a sort of gloom that just was, in which she never questioned why her brothers rarely left the farm and then only at nightfall, why they never had a sweetheart, why her father with his top boots, waistcoat, watch chain and chin whisker had an aura of silent threat broken by periods of histrionic, brutal blind drunkenness, why her mother sometimes read the Bible all night and considered Elmira, even as a child, to be evil and impure and left bruises on her back and thighs from the fire poker so that she couldn't even turn over at night. Nor why her mother cut the boys' hair with a bowl on their heads so they were shaved above the ears like monks in picture books, instead of going to the barber, why her brothers kept appearing in court in Leith or for a week in the lock-up, why she wasn't allowed to go to the dances. By the age of fifteen, however, she did question the murky untying, unbuttoning, rubbing and groping she had carried on with her brothers like animals thrown together in ignorance in the dark, vaguely initiated, perhaps, by a faceless older person. The only one who left her alone was Elmer who was massive and deaf and moved about like a dumb circus elephant. In the end, she had fended off her drunken elder brother Isaac with a stick of firewood and he had to say the bloody cut and black eye had come from the Edderfield boys. Daily, she reassured herself that it had been with the ash-gatherer that she'd lost her virginity at fourteen.

She hauled wood, milked cows, scrubbed floors, raked hay, threshed grain, walked behind a plough and a harrow, drove a hay wagon with the rest from dawn to dark when she sewed patches and repaired shoes and harness in dim candlelight when her father was too cheap to get kerosene or had spent everything on whisky and she sat all winter beside the stove, reading to her parents with difficulty from the newspaper, her dress patched so often, she only had two dreams, to get a new dress and to be with Tom.

One September she was up to her elbows in blood, scraping out a hog, when she spied him out on the road and he seemed the cause of all the wildflowers around him, tall and ambling in a made-up suit, part homespun, with a waistcoat and topcoat, and a face that reddened easily, and a hat tilted back on stiff, greased black hair. She heard he'd been shirking work at home and was being beaten for it and soon she found grown-up ways of heading him off but he was polite and silent, doubtless because he was intelligent and still he had that bearing of solitude and nobility. And then she saw him being ridiculed by the girls at the Leith-Connemara crossroads because he claimed to know more than the school teacher when he hadn't even a decent pair of boots and that was when she married him in her mind.

In the meantime she found another boy, Tim Croxall, and then Abe Farley. When she brought Farley home, her father and brothers picked a fight with him and ran him off the property and her mother struck her across the face with the Bible, saying no man from outside was ever to set foot there. The exception was the odd travelling salesman that her father would invite to stay over because he had no one to talk to, keeping the man up all night about his exploits in the old days in some feud of which she only heard drunken, incoherent fragments through the floorboards and then he'd hire the man for a week. That way, she had the shirt salesman down by the stream and Wilbur Kent, who sold magic lantern slides, in the driving shed during a blizzard and after he was gone she miscarried. There was slander in Leith that neither visitor had ever left the property and she wondered because she herself had never seen them depart. Still, she defended her family name from the girls who mocked them with the insulting epithet "Craggshaw," perverts and animals in human form, and she learned to bite and scratch and pull hair and then the girls steered clear.

In her heart, she had begun to wonder about something in her family's farm, her birthplace. From a hilltop road or from other farms where she worked, it stood out, a blighted anomaly on a bald ridge, and then on the back hundred the melancholy passage of the Maskinonge Central with its mournful whistle made it even worse, and she swore there had to be a cause for it all, like a disease in the groundwater or deep in the past.

In defence, she despised the stuck-up, beribboned girls all the more, the ones who talked about marrying and money and land and the respectable men to whom they were engaged, none of it being within her grasp. But at least she knew, and still without a mirror, that she could paralyze their gentleman callers at a glance and was more amusing and carefree than the girls who were tied in knots of worry about their future and probity and so, like water seeking its lowest course, she took what she could get by running into some eligible son of Leith and they'd find their way to a creek bottom or a lane or tall-standing grain and she was on her back in ditches after dark, behind barns, in the manger of the church driving shed. She liked the smell of them and feeling them and having them inside her in moments of private paradise – the only thing that wasn't work and death.

The whole time, she found ways of keeping a cow within sight of the line and milking it there so that one day, with the bucket, she managed to get to the road and fall in beside Tom who said he was on his way to the reading room off the billiard parlour in the Grand Hotel in Leith when, in fact, she knew he was being sent to the mill to help his brothers who dumped sacks of flour on his head, kicked him in the backside, pulled chairs out from behind him and tipped him off ladders. As usual, she had to do the talking, her heart thumping wildly. Pretending to leave, she'd speed up or slow down but he stayed with her and she said to herself, "I got him hooked like a fish." They began meeting and walking at odd hours in odd slivers of time but he wouldn't touch her. He recited the constellations, the planets and the books of the Old Testament. He told her about Homer, Moses, Alexander the Great, Confucius, Louis Napoleon and the Tsar Nicholas and the Sultan of Turkey, saying he had a secret source of knowledge but she knew that most of it had come from the newspaper and the almanac. She talked about the people they knew but he wouldn't say much probably because he was a pariah, even in his own family, so other people, in general, were a burden. He preferred facts and theories and mused about the world with the air of a detached witness to great and tragic events.

As it began to rain one day, he said, "It's not going to last. Them factories in the city, all that smoke, it's poisoning the air.

All the new industries and inventions are destroying nature. People laugh at the automobile. They say it's a luxury, a joke. But automobiles, they have their own smoke and there will be thousands of them diseasing everything in ways that are invisible, like this generation which is mentally more feeble than the generation past. We will destroy the very air itself. The sky will turn green and the sun will turn red, and a vapour will settle over the land. People's faces will turn grey and bleed from the mouth and eyes. It's coming. In our lifetime or that of our children," and she thought, The only children I'd ever be able to keep would be with him, anyway. It was suppertime and the road ahead was empty, they'd be alone a while yet.

"And what about Craggshaws," she teased him, "Are they real too?"

"The Craggshaws are like the Titans. From the *Iliad* and the *Odyssey*. They're a legend."

"So we're all going to die before our time," she said.

"Things were at their best twenty years ago. Round here at any rate. About 1880. Our forefathers who made this land out of the bush. Now it's all cleared, it's being destroyed."

"How's it worse now?" she said,

"First thing, in 1885, they took the railroad away from Leith because they claimed they could save money with a route through Connemara station between Toronto and Orillia but it was all politics and money and now Leith is a dying town," and it occurred to her then that her grandpa Rawlinson had been part of it, selling a tract of land off the farm for the 1885 railroad allowance and there had been some kind of scandal.

The rain was coming down harder now and he just walked in it, showing no desire to take her anywhere and she racked her brain and could only think of Manley's cow shed up ahead. It would be full of cows but there was a spot under the eaves that couldn't be seen from the road and she said, "I know a place out of the rain."

"All right," he said.

But then the rain stopped and she thought a little and said, "I want to show you the view there anyway."

It was a bleak field of mud. The eaves were leaking and they were up to their ankles in a mire of cow dung and urine, lakes of acrid-smelling amber liquid. She held his arm and encouraged him to get close and then he was kissing her and as his hand got up her dress and into her knickers she imagined a church wedding and loosened the strings so he could go further up or down and she was feeling him too, half his trouser buttons were missing anyway. There was a place where the mire and manure was drier and as the rain started again, she tried to pull him down there and he stumbled, falling against her, the two leaning toward the excrement, but he wouldn't go down, seeming to think himself too refined for that and hauled her back up and they got her knickers down to her knees but his breeches were held too high, so together they wrestled his jacket off one arm at a time so it wouldn't fall in the mire and then unbuttoned his vest so they could get his suspenders down and then she helped him get inside her, the two standing up, wobbling and moving in a blinding downpour.

She didn't get home until after dark, and when she got in they were still around the table, in silence, waiting. Normally her mother would have beaten her but there had never been a terrible silence like this and her mother said, "You're not gettin' nothin'." And her father said, "You do that again, you'll die."

"Do what again?" she said.

The brothers, except for Elmer who was deaf, burst out laughing. She sat down before her empty plate and they stared at her. They must have known who it had been and something about him. As if it had been carried on an evil wind.

She was no longer sent on errands or to other farms and at home she was always watched by at least one of the other six and, sensing no real explanation, she resorted to eavesdropping. As the leaves fell and the wind shook the house, as the first flurries weaved on the biting air and she repaired overcoats and patched rank, stained long johns, as ice formed on the fields and pools of lantern light swung through the stables, as she lit the stove days on end and her brother Isaac stared at her non-stop, she picked up fragments from mundane arguments when, for example, her mother threatened her father with an axe, or a midnight squabble and stabbing among her brothers, and a picture materialized: the old grandfather had obtained the back hundred in 1884 from an absentee landlord for almost nothing through bribery and deceit; after selling the tract to the CPR for a fortune, the elderly Rawlinson, who was then being sued for defrauding the banks, had hidden the money on the property before hanging himself, dying intestate and loathing his family, leaving each of her parents and four brothers in a terrible solitude, privately convinced that one or more of the others knew where the money was, or pretended they knew or didn't know, even at knifepoint. The wainscotting in the house had been jimmied, there'd been digging around the property, the granary floor had been torn up, stones removed from the barn foundation.

Now she understood the lunatic economy by which her father ran the farm: borrowing to enlarge the property on the dream of having an estate ready to exploit when the money came to light or whenever he could safely recover it, now forced to keep it all under production to pay the appalling mortgage which explained their chronic destitution and the bleak fire of megalomania that burned in his eyes when he had the jug late at night. His desperation to obtain land while it was supposedly cheap was why the boys had taken to brigandage to supplement the household income and obtain pocket money and why they got into brawls in the bars of Leith. It also explained why her father needed another hand and was faced with the dilemma of bringing an outsider to work on a farm already sick and paralyzed with fear of the outside world.

For a while he had no need to worry: no one in Maskinonge would work for them. The man who finally answered the ad wore white duck trousers, a linen jacket and a boater and was from Toronto. His name was Latimer Davenport and he was given the bedroom where the grandfather had hanged himself. He had soft white hands and used big words that no one understood, and Elmira noticed that when you passed him in the hall there was no smell. For the first week he seemed paralyzed with terror. Nor could he do the work. But he was fair-haired and good-looking and she saw instantly that he was her only hope of leaving the place. She got close to him. He was vague about his origins and told her instead about his interest in making a quick fortune in the mass production of automobiles, in electricity or in a medicine that would cure everything as well as a crystal skull in Mexico that had healing powers proven by science. After her younger brother John was shot and wounded one night in the kitchen, Davenport came down in the morning and vomited at the sight of him being held down by his brothers on the kitchen table while his mother dug out the bullet and sewed him up. Only by telling the new man about the hidden fortune did Elmira get him to stay, and then only barely. He worked half-heartedly and picked at the blisters on his hands before she took him to the back fields where they'd sit down and try to ascertain where the money was and who knew. In November, they were digging turnips and had intimate relations. Otherwise, he remained mysterious.

It was by steaming open his mail that she found out about him and became so engrossed that she finished learning to read, acquiring grammar and enlarging her vocabulary through the eloquence and erudition of Davenport's parents and relations, absorbing new words like "wastrel," "effete," "remittance," "appalling," "degenerate." He was neither an engineer nor a chemist as he had claimed. Nevertheless, and most importantly, he came from great wealth, a mining family with a mansion on St. George Street in Toronto. He had grown up lazy, frivolous, and incompetent. He'd forged doctors' prescriptions to obtain opium. Now, with an air of moral superiority, she opened more letters about his parents having to pay off his debts, about bringing shame on the family. His father had answered the ad for farm labour and sent him to earn his way by the sweat of his brow up in Maskinonge, despite the township's aura of scandal and depravity, a reputation of which the residents were unaware.

As she bound sheaves from the feeble swathes that Davenport tore and crushed with the scythe, she touched indirectly on matters in his correspondence to see what more she could gain without divulging her invasion of his privacy until one day he remarked, "If you'd properly read the letter from my mother of August 6th, about my debts, it completely contradicts the one from Uncle Jack on the 2nd, the one about the bank loan." From the first day on the farm, it turned out, he'd had no expectations of anyone.

It was in February, on an errand to town and under escort by Isaac, that Elmira received a shock. The postmaster let slip that Tom's parentage had come into question.

"What do you mean, Craggshaw?" Elmira said, "Craggshaws are monsters, they're a story, aren't they?"

"That's what I thought too," the postmaster said.

The news had already spread like heat lightning. One night when she'd forgotten to lay the morning fire, Elmira came down after midnight. Her father was drunk at the kitchen table and she was about to make a run for it when, for the first time ever, he used her name and then mumbled, "That fella, that fella what's Craggshaw now, you talked to him, right?" She nodded. Uneasily, he told her that Craggshaws had been there in the early days of settlement. They'd been involved in a feud. Mrs. Phair had committed adultery with Ned Craggshaw in 1879 and Tom was the result, the latter only just having learned of his paternity when he inherited a house on the Leith Line. When Tom had also tried to claim the untilled land with the ruined stone foundation across the road, he'd gotten cut up in a knife fight with the man who intended to buy it, a man by the name of Bascomb. Her father looked up at her, and with a tangle of euphemism and arch circumlocution, asked if she had become pregnant by Tom Phair. When she said she hadn't, he looked down in despair.

She kept her ears open, listening in company with a brother or parent, to gossiping midwives and drunken farmers, to mumbling brothers through blizzards thundering around the house. Under heartless blue skies and infinite ceilings of grey she learned about a wicked compact of Tory families that first ran the township, until Craggshaws began to burn them out and prevail through superior skill at arson, assault, battery and electoral fraud until two Craggshaws were murdered, provoking a reign of terror in which the night skies were red from arson and the taverns of Leith ran with blood through the spring and summer of 1877, and Tom's father, the massive Ned Craggshaw, an unsurpassed fighter, beat to a pulp every town constable brought to Leith and induced a threshing boycott in which three Bascomb families lost their harvests. The newspapers throughout the Dominion termed Leith "hell on earth," "the wildest spot in Canada," until, in the winter of 1881, the Craggshaw families were gathered at the homestead for a wedding when seven of them, including Tom's father, were murdered and the house burned by a mob of forty "parties unknown." The surviving Craggshaws were run out of the township. Every soul in Maskinonge was related to one or more of the untried killers and a cloud of shame settled on the district and the past was expunged from memory. In vain, the odd American promoter remonstrated that violence, crime and mob justice were nothing to be ashamed of and ought to be marketed, but the priggish ways of the Dominion prevailed. The story, fragmentary, whispered and mythologized, lasted longer in the rest of Canada than it did in the place where it had happened, the township's 19th-century history now an entirely phony record of respectable farmers and civic pride. The shabby fields and fences and barns slept into the 1890s as people like the Rawlinsons unwittingly kept the real tradition alive at a lower level of depravity and squalor. The old Tory Bascombs ran the township and ensured that the Craggshaws remained a cautionary fairy tale, embalmed in a limbo of the imagination.

On a wild night in March, the elder Rawlinson drew his daughter aside yet again. Convinced more than ever that she had some connection with the revived Craggshaws, he confided that the railway down at the back had been built five years after the massacre on land still owned by Craggshaws, implying that his own father had simply stolen it before bribing the CPR into a slight detour across the land and then selling it as a railway allowance. With the money from the Craggshaw land hidden on the farm, he now feared them like unquiet dead and calculated that appeasement through bonds of marriage was the wisest course. Assuming she shared the family's instinctive greed, he wondered whether Elmira might introduce them to Tom Phair. For the first time in her life an accurate picture of her kin materialized: they had fully participated in the feud but as mercenary cowards and her father's craven, snivelling offer of reconciliation proved once and for all the moral vacuity of her entire family and forebears. In April, while peeling turnips with her mother, she ascertained from the old woman's smirking contempt for her husband that those who had killed the Craggshaws were not entirely nameless, the implication only too clear.

From the house he had inherited, Tom Phair drank and gazed daily at the land across the road and the ruined foundations of the family homestead, the site of the massacre; indeed, the Bascomb with whom he had brawled over the right to purchase was the son of those who had killed his forebears. Around suppertime, Tom would appear on the blasted road that ran down the ridge into town, wearing a fine but outmoded black suit, raging with a sense of ancient entitlement, and demanding redress. From gallery porches and second-floor verandas people looked on in nervous and embarrassed silence. Some hailed him with a greeting of fake cheer as he staggered drunk, challenging all comers with a double-bladed bowie knife. They could only hope he would go away, like a bad dream, a revenant, but instead he became a feature in the taverns where he was served with speed and courtesy. Elmira, accompanied by her mother, pretended not to see him when he stumbled drunk and hollering in the frozen ruts of the main street while her love soared to new heights. He was the aristocratic outlaw she had known all along.

Her distancing from Davenport had already begun. Increasingly, the city man had displayed a fey haughtiness made worse by an even more feminine petulance. When he suggested that she bore no blood relation to her brothers and that if their skulls could be measured with callipers their congenital inferiority could be proven, she beat him and the break was complete. Meanwhile, the old man, irked by his daughter's silence on Tom Phair, came to suspect she had communicated something to the hired man. When he was drunk, the elder Rawlinson had begun to exhibit a strange intimacy with Davenport who'd respond with teasing flirtation until the old man would stumble after him laughing and demented with lust. In the dark of night, Elmira was awakened by a terrible smashing and looked out to see the hired man, with his bag, fleeing into the darkness. Below, her father crawled about, mumbling and bloody, in the shattered kitchen.

With reason now, she dreaded sunset; on another night, as the vapours of spring carried the mournful train whistle, the voices of Isaac and the old man came up through the floor: Isaac was no relation to any of them: as an infant, he had been taken from a church for free labour. If a sense of consanguinity had once held him back, it did no longer. She fled before his advances until finally he forced himself on her in the parlour. She buried a paring knife in his shoulder, but even that wouldn't stop him, and she was saved only when her mother stormed in, hollering that the parlour was only for Sundays. Elmira had reached the limit; they needed a chambermaid at the Grand Hotel in Leith and she risked her life, leaving in the middle of the night with nothing but the clothes on her back.

The Grand had a bar, one of many on the main street subject to the wild bombast and jeremiads of Tom Craggshaw, as he now called himself. Above, she emptied chamber pots and boiled the malodorous sheets of incontinent travelling salesmen and farmers too drunk to go home, rejecting their stumbling, obscene advances in a renewed spirit of saintly purity as she waited, each night, for Tom to appear. On hot summer evenings as the crickets rang, he'd materialize, a black speck moving down the hill on the dirt road into the town. She did shifts as a barmaid downstairs and served him as he stood heroic and alone, his foot on the rail, giving her a faint nod. Toward night, his performance would begin and he'd single out the living murderers from the nameless mob of 1881, rhyming off the twenty-one patronymics, cursing above all the Bascombs who had led them. She stayed as near to him as she could. Even when members of her family were in town, the widespread and deepening fear of the past seemed to keep them away from Tom.

In August he appeared with a revolver, firing it aimlessly around the main street. On an evening a week later, he began to shoot out windows. Frustrated by the town's quiet toler-ance, he called out that Willy Bascomb Junior was an abortion, an abomination and a pervert. By then, Willy and his friends had had enough and he met Tom to fight on the evening of September 2, before a crowd of two hundred spectators, with candy and drinks for the children, the elderly in invalid chairs or carried out on pallets. The two went at it with bare fists and kicking and eventually with knives, stabbing, dragging, hack-ing and gouging, in and out of the bar of the Grand, back and forth across the street until Tom lay on the board sidewalk in a pool of blood, Elmira on her knees pulling him into her arms as Bascomb and his friends went off into the silent, dissolving crowd.

Tom Phair was carried up to a room in the Grand. The doctor did his best, bandaging and sewing, while Tom dulled the pain with a bottle of cherry wine, Elmira holding it to his lips. Pretending mature dispassion, she agreed to tend him until the doctor returned in the morning. The man left and the last of the Craggshaws took her weakly in his arms and even as he began to bleed again, she pulled her dress up and her knickers down and he was soon inside her, hard despite everything, until the utter end when he ceased to move and expired on top of her.

He was buried in the unmarked Craggshaw plot by the church. Elmira missed her time of the month and scrubbed away in the Grand knowing that she carried inside her the living golden age before the world turned bad and she racked her mind to plan it a future. None too soon, she received a letter from Davenport apologizing for the remark about the callipers and asking her hand in marriage. She mailed off her consent and he wrote back, promising to arrive on Sunday in a red Packard at Connemara station, on the highway into Toronto. To Elmira's horror, her only good dress was back at the farm. In the wee hours after Saturday, when everyone was sure to be unconscious, she returned. The fetid old house shook with snoring and the murmur of poisoned dreams as she changed into her dress, packed a bag and got out. And she went off on the road, laying a hand on her stomach, knowing that the old life lived. Under Tom's star.

JOSIAH LOVE

Lucinda's Smoke Shop had once been the parlour of a hotel and was gloomy with a high ceiling of stamped tin and a beaten wood floor and smelled of bubble gum and cheap perfume. The woman for whom the shop was named was getting close to sixty, tall and bulky in a black dress, with thick bifocals and hair like iron and an air of authority as she rang in gum and *Archie Comics* for two girls and four packs of Players for a couple of mill hands from across the street. That was when Josie Love came in with a case of empty pop bottles. She had been living in apprehension of him but now betrayed nothing.

Lucinda counted the pop bottles, rang open the till and gave him two dollars. He sat down in a chair across from the counter, not four feet from the flowered curtain that covered the stairway door to the upstairs apartments, and began to roll a cigarette. He wore baggy beige pants, oversized black work boots, a patched pinstripe suit jacket and a broken hat and his dark half beard made his flat blue eyes unearthly. Lucinda knew what he was thinking as he sat there with his leg crossed, bouncing his boot, decorously setting the cigarette in a standing ashtray that had come from what had been the hotel lobby. In a while, he got up and used the washroom beside the curtained door to the stairs and came back and sat down and eventually he said, "Today's March 18th," and she said, "I'm aware of that." Slowly, she got a sandwich in Saran wrap from a glass case and poured a coffee and set them on the counter. After an interval, he got up to get them and sat down again.

He finished eating and had another cigarette while people came and went and she rang in their purchases and wished to hell he would leave. Eventually he said "Yup," and got up slowly and went out and she heard the iron wheels of the cart he pulled fade away upon the sidewalk. Every week he would gather bottles from the roadside ditch, get the deposit for the beer bottles at Brewer's Retail and for the pop bottles at Lucinda's Smoke Shop and then would walk the four miles back to the township dump where he lived in a shack made from salvaged junk.

He had been married to Lucinda of Lucinda's Smoke Shop for thirty-six years. They had met in 1924 at a Temperance picnic on the corner of the town line and the sixth concession. He had been clean and neat and off liquor for three months according to five men and the more credible testimony of two women. He was a shy man, sitting apart from the others in long dry grass, and had the most gorgeous eyes Lucinda had ever seen, like seas of blue. Later she would say, "Never, ever, marry a man for his eyes," but thirty-odd years later there were still those pools of blue in the haggard face, eyes reflecting the soul of the same man with that quiet, humorous charm, however decayed. She had told him that if he stayed sober for one year, he could move back in with her into the apartment over the store, cautioning him that she could tell if he had taken even one sip in three days. The previous year, he had quit drinking on the 19th and hadn't had a drop since, but she still wasn't entirely sure how far, really, to let him up those stairs, how many actual steps before she would change her mind. It had been a nightmare and could be a nightmare again.

Josiah Love went down in the ditch and picked up a piece of stovepipe and a tire. Tomorrow would be the 19th but he had thought he'd try the 18th just to see if she'd give him the benefit of a single day, but of course it had to be a year to the day, probably even to the minute. That's the way she was. He had not been up that curtained stairway in twenty-nine years.

For much of that time, he had wandered drunk and lain in the woods and on sidewalks, had begged and done odd jobs and slept in the town park until he found he could salvage and repair things in the township dump and sell them at the gate. Eventually he got enough scrap lumber and metal to make a one-room shack right in the dump, by the entrance. Then someone threw out a wood stove which he installed along with discarded stove piping and a four-paned window. He knew from which farms and houses a lot of the trash and decent usable furniture and things came out of and he maintained a sense of authority from the fact that the dump, at Highway 9 and the fourth line, was at the centre of the township and that he had, in effect, become the repository of the past. Slowly, he sorted and organized all the refuse, directed the dumping and sold abandoned chairs, wire, basins, lawn mower parts, kindling and wainscotting, all neatly piled and sorted in a row by the entrance, and sold some of the furniture to wealthy city

people who seemed to think it had some value. Finally, he had .
made the cart for collecting bottles with iron wheels salvaged
from two wheelbarrows and a factory dolly before be put the
frame and box together from metal and scrap wood. Until the
last year, however, he had drunken down whatever he had
managed to make.

He got to the dump, fired up the stove and sat down. His
eye drifted across a corner of the one thing he kept hidden, a
torn, brittle page from an album with an 1879 photograph of
men in grey clothes and wide-brimmed hats set back on their
heads, with moustaches and wide, faded eyes, posing in front of
a team of horses and wagon piled high with sacks of grain from
a record harvest. He had figured out who they were and had
been tempted to fix the picture to the wall beside his shaving
mirror but decided not to. A thought passed of Lucinda who
had already gotten bulky and heavy thirty years ago and was
probably much the same now – big and soft and warm and a little saggy, the great pale breasts and big pink nipples and big
rear end to which he would return, finally passing through that
curtain at the back of the store and up those worn steps.

As night came and he slept, his last fading thought was his
own startling appearance in the world. He had been born in
1900 but as far as he knew, he had simply found himself at age
four standing in a yard looking across to a barn and flat pasture
and a pale sky on the farm of people named Love. And he too
was called Love, just like Ma and Dad and the five other children. He was second youngest and all of them, at some point,
had been served dinner first, except for him and he had always
been the last to be included in any games and they hardly even

used his name. Each one graduated from carrying feed to running the house or midwifing cows and pigs to driving a wagon or ploughing but he was left cleaning out pens and they teased and often beat him. The only good times had been when Auntie Elmira Davenport visited, a tall woman in a blue flowered dress and a big straw hat who was dizzy and scattered and like a child herself and the others said she was crazy but she secretly gave him extra licorice and he had always been included among the two or three she took to town and on picnics. After she left, he would lie awake at night with three other brothers and turn over and away from them and cry, longing for her in silence.

On the morning of March 19th, he heated water from a jerry can and shaved in a basin and embarked on his last trip collecting bottles so that Lucinda would know that he took nothing for granted. It was warm and grey and crows were cawing and it felt like spring. He passed the Love farm, now run by a second cousin who barely said hello. The fourth line ran along a rise of land and the township fell away to the north, the fields sloping down into bare bush before rising again toward the moraines of Leith, Connemara and Saintfield, carrying a half-veiled hundred-year-old past which he'd managed mostly to excise from his mind except that now, on the eve of its final and thankful annihilation, the glimpse of the pale strip of the sixth line, beyond the bush, would not leave him alone. He had worked on a farm there. He'd been about twelve and he and his brothers had heard from neighbours that Bob Craggshaw paid good wages to kids to help with hay or fire wood. His brothers told him not to go because Craggshaw was an evil name but on Sundays when they went fishing, he would defect to a group of other boys who wandered like stray dogs and go with them up to the farm, square and flat with its plain, sturdy house and barn. Mr. Craggshaw was tall and rangy, about seventy, with a straggling moustache and terrifying eyes, faded like distant fire, though he never did anything to the boys. Perhaps that was because they worked hard in excited terror, raking and tying up sheaves, loading the wagon, harnessing and unharnessing the horses, even after they had learned he hired kids because he was widowed and childless which was, in turn, because of some evil in the blood of his family and he'd long been damned to hell. But the old man never did anything but hide their hats or pretend to withhold their wages or surreptitiously poke a boy in the back with his cane and laugh as he watched the boy turn and kick the boy behind him.

When Josiah's parents learned that on Sundays, instead of going fishing he had gone and worked for Craggshaw, his father beat him and locked him for six hours in the granary. But the boy always went back and again he'd be punished. Old Craggshaw, of whom he was still terrified, paid him a little more than the others and told him to keep quiet about it and sometimes talked with him. Secretly, he decided Mr. Craggshaw was all right but still, he was nervous about the evil that was said to reside in him.

Josiah knew vaguely that Craggshaws had been a bad family, a blight long ago annihilated from the township, but he was unsure if the old man was of the same Craggshaws. They were said to be from up around Leith, on the Oak Ridge, and were now unremembered and without faces, no image, no clothing, no aspect, not even any names. Just incoherent tales and dying rumours of a dark age of squatting on land, burning barns, conflating enterprise with highway robbery, knifing, burning and beating, until they had bought up half the township, resisted only by their rivals, the Bascombs. Then, in 1881 a tidal reaction of rural virtue, God and temperance rose out of the soil and six Craggshaws were murdered by parties unknown and the name Craggshaw vanished, not just from the side roads leaving empty, ruined farms, but from memory itself. Their mention evoked only a quick and dark privation; the patronymic submerged in night and without faces or given names but ever afterward an object lesson, a simulacrum of evil.

Old Mr. Craggshaw was said to be insane, at worst an aging pervert rumoured to have committed murder; and by the time of that younger generation, born around 1900, he was a figure of fear and rumour. And then the boys noticed the subtle preference that the old man showed for Josie Love until it was said that old Craggshaw was queering him and that was when Josie, who had never known the reasons for the old man being kind to him, started getting into side road fights with those who had insulted both him and the old man. Josie lost almost all of them, but and over and over he told the stories of the few fights he had won.

Lucinda Love sold a *Toronto Daily Star*, two bottles of milk, four sandwiches, three Cokes and a Pepsi and was thinking if Josiah came in sober and decent no earlier than four o'clock that afternoon, she would most probably let him up through the curtain at eight when she closed up. The next step would be a bath and the clean clothes she had bought two days before. She had always been fastidious. That was how she gave out credit, how she allowed rent upstairs to be owed with daily interest up to one month before eviction.

Love noted some wire in the ditch and picked up another pop bottle and went on. He passed a field too evenly ranked with oaks and maples, the site of a tavern. Forty-odd years before, there had been bars at every couple of crossroads, vanished dens of sin and violence, and he had been having a drink in the building that had been there among those trees when he was still in his teens. That wild early spring night of cold mud in 1917, he had been asked by Will Bascomb Junior if the old queer fellow, Craggshaw, had rigged him an exemption from serving in the War. A table was smashed and upended and Josie had yanked the leg off and he had Bascomb on the floor and was beating him and there was blood all over the place before Bascomb stuck him nine times with a jackknife, laying Josie up for two weeks in a room in the tavern, since his father decided then and there and finally, not to take him back. The War ended and they brought in prohibition. The taverns were closed as if they had been infected with too much evil and had to be purged, and they crumbled and fell into the long grass and disappeared and, in some ineffable way, the whole countryside became empty. He was working around the farms as itinerant labour when a letter or Christmas card from Auntie Elmira would find its way to him and twice he met her at a soda parlour in town. She was heavier now, but still in the blue dress and straw hat and she still loved him and he broke down and told her that he had taken the pledge and that he missed her.

He worked on, underfed, cheated of wages, jilted by girls, lying with them when he could, in a barn or roadside, or for an hour in a room over a tavern, expecting he would die the way he lived, until one day an errand boy from a lawyer found him with a threshing gang on a place near Saintfield and told him to come to the law office.

He was greeted by a lawyer, J.S. Crist, and also by a registrar, notary public and secretary. He thought he was going to be arrested. He would remember that day, June 17, 1924, when he walked out of that office and went to collect his belongings at the farm where he'd been working and then up toward Leith, to take possession of a farm already overgrown – old Mr. Craggshaw having died six months before without notification or funeral nor any known burial plot. He had simply vanished and the farm was Josie's and now he took a scythe to the grass around the house, trying still to apprehend that Auntie Elmira Davenport was his mother. Old Mr. Craggshaw, who had employed him had been his great uncle; and his grandfather, Edward Craggshaw, had done time for arson and publicly beaten bloody three successive town constables in front of crowds of a hundred on the main street of Leith between 1876 and 1880 before dying in the massacre in 1881. His son Tom wandered, wifeless and childless, trying to sustain his family's name with a drunken hellishness that people now watched from gallery porches with guarded patience. And one night, Elmira Rawlinson, then a chambermaid, tended his knife wounds in a hotel in Saintfield and lay with him and conceived Josiah before Tom Craggshaw was himself beaten to death with the bar of a grain balance. Pregnant, Auntie Elmira had eloped with a city man by the name of Davenport, so that Josiah had been born in Toronto only to be placed in an orphanage. When he had turned three, his mother picked him up and left him, unofficially, at the farm of friends called Love and not even the Loves knew who the father had been. "Now you are, in theory, the last Craggshaw," the lawyer had told Josiah gently, "and I would recommend you keep that more or less to yourself and retain the name Love. If you want to get ahead."

Approaching town now, he pulled the cart along and saw an empty Hires Root Beer bottle in the ditch and speculated that it was probably the last empty bottle he would ever pick from the roadside. And again, the image opened before him of those three worn steps under the curtain that hung over the door, leading upward to a place from which he had fallen and to which he would return, to the cooking and the warmth and those big, warm white breasts and backside. He'd even heard that she had obtained a television.

Back then, he had hoped to farm but on the old Craggshaw place he had had no woman or family and had to recruit help where he could find it and as he worked on, usually alone, the name lodged deep but awkwardly inside him as if it were stuck to a rib or the bottom of his esophagus, and when he cut himself and saw the blood in the grain stubble or on the barn floor he would feel the strangeness of his own diseased atoms. In those days, he had come to recognize a certain path that opened off from a side road, like a dark nothingness in the green wall of bush, and he could pass it several times without stopping before he'd relent and go into the heart of the swamp to the worm and the tubs, the mash and the furnace, and pay fifty cents for a jug of clear, liquid fire. He fought it and managed to stay away from the bush path. Then heard that Auntie Elmira, the woman who was his mother, had died and he lay down and wept in a half-harvested field and the next day went back to the swamp. He worked and slept drunk and the farm became rundown. The bank seized it and he used the remaining cash to buy the still.

He could never tell who knew he carried the mark, the stigma, and who didn't know, and those dark windy gaps in the mind of the township he could only obliterate with corn liquor which he sold and drank, living in the former bootlegger's hut on cold corned beef hash eaten from the tin with a spoon. One morning, a Methodist minister materialized out of the dense green at the hut in the swamp and told him that God knew all the twists and turns and secrets of his soul but loved him anyway. Two weeks later, he had abandoned the still and lived through the sweats and hallucinations and horrors, lying in agony in fields and bush when he stripped and washed himself in a stream and put on the clean clothes the minister had given him and went to the Temperance picnic.

There, he noticed a woman he had seen in town and nodded to but who had always scared him. She was tall, commanding and buxom and had a figure. Lucinda Usher was a little dark, maybe like an Italian, but she radiated power and had that rosy-cheeked assurance, the ebullience of the female devotee of Temperance. He wondered how he could get her attention, and the only things he could come up with were tapping her on the back and ducking behind a tree or stealing her hat.

But she was already approaching him, dark and magnificent, a tall, iron silhouette against a wild sunset to the redemptive trill of crickets. She advised him that he had chaff stuck to the brilliantine in his hair and he quickly wiped it off with a handkerchief and she asked him to join the group for a last sandwich and lemonade. A year later they were married in the Methodist church in Connemara and she took his name, Love. That he was the last issue of Craggshaws had remained the well-kept secret of the lawyer and the registrar. And anyway, Josiah decided he was a Love and Lucinda always insisted that his people, the Loves, were fine people, for cousins of Loves had always neighboured and changed farm work with her own people, the Ushers.

A childless aunt died, willing Lucinda the proceeds of her farm and she bought the hotel. Josiah turned his own hand to it and fixed it up and by 1929 had a position: in a suit and tie behind the front desk, signing in guests or meeting them at the train station with a wagon and team while he and Lucinda saved for a truck. They lived in a small house in town but after a few years, and despite resolute efforts to have a child, the seed never took. What he did not understand was the fear that kept growing under his sadness. In rage repressed into tearful indignation, Lucinda kept saying, "I'm normal, that I know," and slowly he became convinced that he carried what he told himself was "the curse of Leith," the seed which, instead of germinating, killed and rendered barren the place where it fell, conceiving an absence, a privation. Until one day, when he was driving the wagon along the town line he found himself stopped and it was that gap in the bush, that darkness preceded by a faint path over fallen fence. And he went in and the worm and the tub and the mash were still there, only now there was a new fellow running it and something inside Josiah said, "Fine, I am a Craggshaw," and he paid fifty cents for the bottle of clear fire, his first taste in seven years. Those words echoed faintly now, as he approached within a mile of Lucinda's Smoke Shop.

The hands moved toward four o'clock on her wristwatch. She sorted a shipment of *Archie* and *Superman* comics and *Popular Mechanics* into the display rack, sold a carton of Export A, three ham and cheese sandwiches and an Orange Crush, told two little girls they had spent far too much time at the bubble gum machine and sent them home. She reminded herself that she would not even risk living through what she had lived through before – the drunkenness, the smell, the violence, the profanity – then told herself he'd been sober and thought of the eyes from heaven, the bashful humour. Thirty-one years ago, when she had come in to find him with liquor on his breath signing guests into the hotel, only a wall away, it had been the last straw. The hotel had been her pride and now her husband was receiving the guests drunk and telling them off-colour jokes. His comportment with the closing of the railroad line and the paving of Highway 9 spelled the end and she shut the hotel and converted it into apartments and a smoke shop. When Josiah had started to come upstairs at dawn, belligerent and foul-smelling, she barred him and later told him, "You can come back when you have been sober a year."

He had been in the dump ten years when she went to what had become, officially, the United Church Annual Picnic but which she still considered the Temperance Picnic. There had appeared a blonde, gangly, non-stop-talking city woman, named Jenny Crist, who assumed right off that everyone was her friend. She had moved into the area with her husband, a stockbroker named Michael Crist, the son of the lawyer, J.S. Crist. It was a balmy late summer day with crickets and tall standing dry pasture and Lucinda was sitting by the bank of a stream having Sara Lee coffee cake and tea from a thermos when Jenny Crist appeared with her confident, clumsy, wide-footed stride. Only a week before, she had trumpeted her arrival by making a large donation to the church and now, out here, hadn't the sense to stick with one person or group and listen before she opened her mouth but instead moved around from group to group, talking in a continuous stream, saying, "There are the most incredible stories in this area. No one preserves things like that in the city; we're losing the oral tradition there. You people are so incredible!" and now she was sitting not far from Lucinda, her voice ringing out: "One old fellow in the area, I think he's one of the Loves, it turned out he was adopted and that he was really a Craggshaw, that tragic family that were apparently black sheep up at Leith." No one betrayed anything but simply squinted at her, shading their eyes, looking at her in appalled disbelief as she continued: "This woman, Elmira Rawlinson, she's dead now, had him with the son of, I think it was Edward Craggshaw who was one of those that passed away in that unfortunate incident. And she left him with the Loves over here on the fourth line and no one even knew."

"Sounds a little bit off, if you ask me," one of the women said.

"Oh no. My husband heard it from my grandfather when he practised law here and he found out from Harold Soames who was the registrar."

There was some murmuring and a few laughs and some-one said, "Well, isn't that something?"

It was as if nothing had ever been said and, in fact, nothing changed. Lucinda carried on in the smoke shop and Josie Love kept delivering pop bottles and her friends went on saying hello to her and gossiping on the phone. But when she was alone or lay awake at night, there was now something about the man who came to the store every few days, as if he carried a stone inside him, something that could not be removed or broken down; a bloody shadow that had once been in her bride-bed and left her womb dead. And still it moved two or three times a week along the fourth line and where the dump had once been his earthly penance, it now seemed a smouldering Ge-henna and she prayed to Jesus that she not think this way because it was wrong. But still, there were the blue lights of his eyes, and somewhere the clean humility of the man she had met that day in that field, with his hat hung on his knee.

It was five past four. She unpacked a carton of Campbell's soup and arranged it on the shelf and heard the sound of the iron wheels on the walk. The shadow appeared in the door. He had the usual cardboard box of pop bottles. He had shaved but she wondered now whether he simply intended, unaccount-ably, to go away with the deposit money. She counted out the bottles and removed the deposit money from the till without looking at him, uncertain as to whether this time he would hold out his hand for it. He didn't, which made her flinch a little and hold the money in the air a moment and place it in a neutral space on the counter. He walked away from the deposit and sat in the chair across from her with his hands folded, his leg crossed, bobbing his boot, his eyes passing over the space of worn steps under the curtain four feet away. She gave him a sandwich and a coffee.

By five-thirty, it had been the longest he had ever remained in that chair. By six, she was sweeping up. She locked the door and turned out the lights. She went over and drew back the curtain, revealing the stairs, fully illuminated in twilight from the window on the landing. He remembered the window. The stairs suddenly seemed like stairs in a book he'd recovered in the dump, stairs that led up a pyramid to a human sacrifice. He followed her up. Her slip swayed a little below her dress. Up her legs was darkness. The apartment was more or less as he remembered it. She started a bath running and said to him, "You may as well clean up and dress in them clothes there. They're new." He went in and washed and dressed in the new clothes.

She sat in her easy chair and he sat on the sofa while they watched television and had coffee and cookies as Ed Sullivan welcomed a team of acrobats from Austria. A man raised himself standing on his forefinger.

"I'll be danged, look at that, eh?" he said.

"Yup," she said.

Ed Sullivan swivelled stiffly and applauded. They stared at the television. In the minds of both, although in different ways, the archaic image of Leith, six miles to the northwest, burned with a low, sepulchral, phosphorescence in the gathering darkness of evening. Two teams of dogs in numbered shirts played soccer with their noses as the audience applauded. From the corner of his eye he could see down the short hall to the bedroom door that stood ajar, revealing the foot of the bed. He waited. She took off her glasses and rubbed her eyes and put them on again. Her faced, bathed in the pale light of the television, was beautiful.

"You may as well get ready," she said. "There's pyjamas on the table in the washroom." He went in and changed into the pyjamas, came back and saw the sofa made up with sheets, a pillow and blankets. The hall was dark, the bedroom door ajar.

For two months she made up the sofa and he went on sleeping on it, sometimes looking down through the dim space of the bedroom door whence he could hear the faint creak as she turned over in her sleep. One morning, she was up and making breakfast and tried several times to waken him, there on the sofa, and called the doctor. His pulse was gone.

She buried him alongside the Loves in the cemetery. At the small wake she held with her friends, they all had coffee and tea but she allowed no one to sit on the sofa. That evening she covered it in clear plastic. She never washed his sheets.

The following day she went out to the shack in the dump to dispose of his last possessions and found the photograph of the men in grey work clothes and moustaches and huge-brimmed hats tilted back on their heads, posing by the wagon piled high with sacks of grain; they had those flat, distant eyes, eyes that were wild and faded and violent. She laid it in the refuse fire and watched it smoulder until it burned and rose in the air in floating flags of black cinders, gone and annihilated.

THE STREET

The street is empty and there is a silence like none in fifty years, everyone gone while I alone refuse to go, can't say why, something about the place itself, even with a few houses here and there bombed to ruins. Perhaps I will die here, I've never imagined dying anywhere else; even when I was travelling and living abroad, having sworn never to come back, I had not imagined dying in any other place; and equally, when I was four or five I'd never thought of living anywhere else. Perhaps I had always wanted to return, to live here in the place I have, at the same time, hated, reviled for so long. And so I came back, returned to the top floor of the corner house, it looked in all directions on rooftops and trees, on the old neighbourhoods. Wendy, the woman I married, was dying and I was looking after her there, in the north bedroom. Having known periodic poverty and malnutrition all her life, she had never cared much about the future, was mirthful even as she died, still had traces of the red hair and freckles despite the listlessness and pallor. Facing the window, she saw the sky during the day and the constellations at night. The present calamity, the so-called end of the West, it was all on radio, television, on the monitor before the images disintegrated and you couldn't tell whether the proliferation of black-and-white newsreels and old radio voices fogged by a hundred years of static were jamming and disinformation or simply part of the breakdown, a sort of terminal, electronic dementia. And then it all went black and silent and the warning came to get out. The streets and houses emptied and her eyes were dead, illuminated by the dawn, and I buried her in the sunless, grassless backyard and returned to that top floor which had long ago been my aunt's apartment. It was there that I'd come as a child to escape my parents; it was where I now stood in the window regarding the dust-filled conflagration of twilight and wondered about the whole eventide of civilization. Years before, we'd been in another house when Wendy had left me and I'd gone abroad. I'd inherited this corner house and another house three doors up and had rents collected from both, never expecting to return, cursing the memory of the place, repudiating the city as a grimy red-brick backwater, its legions of ramshackle verandas, its vinyl siding and tin window frames, its unique dreariness. But above all, I abhorred this street, dreaded it, the whole two blocks in a forgotten corner of the heart of the city which I feared, loathed in nightmares, a place in which even the light at sunset was poisonous. Nor had I thought I'd find Wendy again; she wrote me that she was in straits and I came back and took the third-floor apartment. It was she who brought me back to a place I would otherwise have refused, would have cut my throat rather than return, and to a house which itself sickened me. Now, at least, my work sustains me through the specter of annihilation as I collate data to determine once and for all if the juggernaut, the insatiable monster of Progress has been worth it in view of the huge losses incurred by its appetite; in fact this, precisely, has been my work: to ask whether things were not better, in aggregate, at various points past along the so-called ascent of the rectilinear Zoroastrian-Judeo-Christian time scale that we call history. Say at some point or points over the last two centuries before the sky acquired its distinctly chemical tint at dawn and sunset, before the purges of peoples, before a pinkish-grey wash replaced the heavens, before the air smelled of something rather than nothing, before summers roasted and the other seasons were reduced to an insipid continuum. My hatred of the street, meanwhile, is partly related to unpleasant things that happened here. But it's also connected to a fear that once back I would be unable to tear myself away again. And now it has happened. And I remain. Even under threat of capture, interrogation, torture and execution. Of course the street isn't all bad with its modest, fat-pillared single gable dwellings mixed with Richardsonian Romanesque half mansions, sandstone oak leaf bas reliefs, corbels and tile, turrets, lintels, arches, pillars, the carved, closely-worked two-storey verandas and balustrades which in brief moments recall an oddly distorted Haiti, medieval Turkey or Egypt, or Renaissance Italy. Not to mention the rooms I've known in the area due to the circumstances of my upbringing, other rooms in other houses looking onto alleys, roofs or other windows, trees at night and sometimes even the Pleiades and then back home with a dying and sanguinary sun in the evening leaking through windows from a vile garden and descending the dining-room walls like a receding inundation of blood. No, my reluctance to leave is nothing I can put my finger on, save one thing: the distant sound of the train that ran across the north end of the street when my best friend Stephen and I were little and played in the yards, the soporific rush and whisper of the passing freight which got me to sleep. That, and other things yet unidentified, prevent me from leaving, from heeding the printed warnings dropped from above, not that Wendy had cared either way, it was the late-evening narcotic whisper and the plangent wail of the horn from long before, I believed I'd heard it when I was born, perhaps even before, in darkness, had certainly heard it well before my final diagnosis. Defective was the word my father had used, the tone of candid, exasperated resignation passed down from the 19th century and refined by the War and the Depression. I couldn't have been more than fifteen with stiff, un-washed hair, my grimy winter ski coat, my pigeon toes, my lack of affect, an uneven precociousness in astronomy and art, an affinity for odd aspects of quantum physics and a complete failure to grasp the fulcrum or volume as displacement of water. My preoccupation with cloud and sunlight, my academic failure, the absence of interest in other people and complete lack of regard for my appearance suggested autism, while the headaches and black-outs and flashes of ecstasy and the roaring in the ears pointed to brain damage or epilepsy – conditions from which I am still not entirely free as I wait, wondering about the end. In addition, my contentment with my aunt's apartment, still furnished as she had left it, stands as proof that I have been succumbing to something all at once satisfying, terrible and helpless especially since the rooms had been a refuge from my exacting parents who had, once they'd acquired the money, adopted with silent ferocity a style that can only be called patrician – a serene insistence on polished silver and brass, damask, chinoiserie, wallpaper with gold and white Persian motifs or the shadowless perfection of the Chinese landscape. While the third floor had been a refuge, my aunt, an observant Roman Catholic, evinced all of the liberality and compassion and none of the horror, sadism, hatred, hypocrisy and violence associated with the religious orders. She recoiled at cruelty, unwitting of the fact that it was in cruelty that the Church excelled. There were, and as far as I know still are, three or four Virgins in the apartment, veiled and unveiled in blue and white with and without the Infant, painted or cast on walls, chests, tables. In those six rooms looking out on the city, nothing impinged, things felt right and normal which is odd since I knew nothing of the right or the normal. She put me up as often as she could. But now, living on the next floor down, there is almost nothing left as I ask myself, Why don't you run now, go to the safe zone or get out of the country while there is still a corridor? But the sound of the train and other more important, indeed insistent things still unidentified come back along with the irony that it is because of the railway that the area was evacuated, the Dupont line just to the north where oil terminals, weapons factories and depots were recently situated, all along the tracks, the entire zone a target; officials even came to the door. Certainly there is little to be lost now in the general collapse since everything in peacetime had become temporary anyway, a matter of convenience, of short-term contract, of survivalism, the false freedom of expediency and transience. The rumbling of bombardment rose in the night, the street endowed for the first time ever with history, the city itself soon to acquire the gloomy grandeur of

Berlin, Tokyo, Dresden, Baghdad, the historical lobotomy of the firestorm. I'd stand at night by Wendy's empty bed listening as the bombardment moved along the rail line to the north, itself like a freight train. From the top of the outside stairs by the kitchen, the senseless illumination of the sky, the clouds of fire, the lurid, burning columns of darkness, the fire-winds approaching from the north and west even as the high bass-wood blossoms still lit the dining room from the east, the bombardment rolling close until the last bits of reception were gone along with the web, whereupon I printed off all my work and the lights went out, and after the ripping howl and blast of the fighter-bombers the phone was gone. There wasn't much left in the refrigerator or the pantry. I was rationing myself on the last of the bread when everything shook and the place was filled with dust and splinters. One corner of the apartment and the roof had been ripped away, the settling of the dust briefly disclosing the stars of Pisces as I moved whatever candles, sheets, clothes and books down a flight to where I am now, the old man, my tenant gone, the big rooms I had not seen for so long empty-feeling, dusty but still dark green with bay windows. And furnished as they had always been. I tried the black rotary phone which the old man had continued to use, the line hissing with static and an odd and distant murmur of 1930s dance music. He'd been an academic and protégé of my Uncle Edgar who had himself been a scholar and diplomat, living and dying here thirty years before, a sullen man with stiff white hair in a soiled green dressing gown, the arms of his glasses stuck upward above his ears. His typewriter was still there. Under various guises Uncle Edgar had caused things to happen in

Africa and in Indochina, in Whitehall, the State Department and in Beijing. Edgar was cold and impersonal but this place too had come as a relief from home since he ignored my fixations, introversion and general obtuseness; it was he who taught me enough to try out my near-useless aptitudes in the world. Even as the bombing comes close, I'm able to work on the typewriter using my own books and his which had remained in shelves in the threadbare sitting room on the east side which faces the street, the street from which, least of all now, have I been able to tear myself, even as the candlelight strains my eyes in the evening. The air assault has stopped quite suddenly, enabling me to take some air and I move up the street, passing the other house where I have a tenant, a wide brick house with shutters: farther up, rats scramble in the heaps of brick from half-wrecked houses and the torrent of a broken water main. Further along, the house of my childhood friend Stephen remains intact but the sudden calm and the increase of devastation toward the tracks presages, of course, an invasion. Even now, as I look out through the ruins, the air still and ionized like the air before a thunderstorm, I ponder my own progress toward an end which seems, in its desultoriness and tendency toward decline, to have mimicked history. I take advantage of the silence to wander farther afield in search of food, the lull recalling the Saturday morning quiet of childhood with nothing but the cawing of crows, for they caw now as they did then, though on the main streets the stores are boarded up or looted so that I'm reduced to looking through whatever houses I can get into. It's night when I obtain entry into what was once Mr. Molnar's house next door. Having fled during the Hungarian Revolution, Mr. Molnar had believed nuclear war imminent, there had been talk of a bomb shelter. And in the basement I find, behind a pile of doors and storm windows, a safe room stacked with imperishable foods from the 1950s – Campbell's soup, Argentina corned beef, Corn Flakes and other comestibles – which, with the use of a bowl and a pot, Edgar's fireplace and debris for fuel allow me to remain where I am. Late one evening, a gentle knock at the door. I recognize a beautiful face. Though two years older than I, she's one of those self-care women, forever going to the gym, the chiropractor, the massage therapist, Reiki and all the rest. She'd spied me from a distance and asks if I was picking garbage in the ruins. I say certainly not and offer her Corn Flakes, tinned beef and water which she politely declines. Her name is Bev. She's trying to persuade me to get out. There was a time when I would have followed her anywhere, she'd been one of the faraway beautiful older girls from around the block, I'd longed for her, it seems, since infancy; but not even the memory of that hot evening excitement and fevered dying light which in children is that wild, nameless longing, diminished and reified as romance in adulthood and which, however urgently recalled, has no hope of pulling me away from the street. "You're facing certain death," she says as I offer her crackers and water. For much of my life, once or twice a year, I'd spy her in the street, watching her become a woman and never ceased to be astonished, and went on to observe her in the odd supermarket or pharmacy after I returned from abroad and now I sense that she's reaching out in a belated attempt to revive some old comradeship, some deep, if elusive meaning from the past and urges me to come along with her. By dark I am once again alone, though I have to admit that the loves I'd pursued had indeed always been far away, around the world or around the block, the same either way. Back near the beginning, on my tricycle, I'd watch a woman at the next corner west, her small mock-Tudor house still visible from the window behind me, a beautiful woman from the cover of a Signet paperback; and a man with a cap and glasses in a red sports car would arrive and she'd get in and when I didn't see them any more I believed that his car had flown away, taking her into the west, the land of Christie Pits and the world beyond. The idea had always been to follow them to where the violet horizon met the evening sky, to escape from home, later taking actual refuge with my aunt or with Uncle Edgar, particularly when I'd become a shambling, friendless nonentity in a Catholic high school. I had then begun reading history at Uncle Edgar's, the same books in the same bookcases that face me now. History has not changed that much. It was there, from Edgar's window, in my awful adolescent years, that I'd look out at dusk and gaze at the vanishing points of dark streets where I sensed the barest glimmer of a future; or from my aunt's windows upstairs faint, nearly nonexistent lights beyond the darkening horizon or even the nearly absent pulse of the farthest stars a million years in the past, perhaps now dead. These gave me hope. Or perhaps something approaching hope. Anything, as long as it was far away. It was at Edgar's that I found Rimbaud, not the poetry so much as the getting away as far as possible, being a trader in Ethiopia; even an early death from amputation in Marseille would have seemed a triumph. Typing now on a manuscript about the disintegration of progress into mere change, rewritten so often that manuscript has itself become a palimpsest, a palimpsest of text, the record of overlapping histories. The sum of which is devoid of anything sustained, certainly not Democracy much less Justice which long ago ceased to be ends, rather had become means to ends long lost to view, ends which I have little choice but to summarize in a vague notion – *the sublime* – of which the synecdoche is the volcano. Not the Beautiful or the Good, no, solely the astonishing and the terrible. Drama and nothing else. The pleasure in comedy and tragedy. In short, delight in catastrophe, failure. Preferably in others. Spectacle. Horror. Sensation. Apocalypse, romantic suffering. Malicious gossip, fire, blizzard, blood, twilight, passion, sadness, *schadenfreude*. The strange beauty of destruction and of course here as well, on this very street. Pleasures which require only freedom. The sole value. Freedom to flirt with death, to love blindly or stupidly, to exult in pain. But also beauty; aesthetics but without moral content or obligation. Mere contentment had never been enough for the late West, the failure of Robespierre's Good Sans-Culottes blindly repeated in Dick and Jane. And now, back in the very room where I came of age and struck outward only to return, I am headed, it seems, even farther back into that from which I came. I hear something, engines from somewhere. An hour later I watch a soldier moving up the street as if he were alone, doubtless a scout, a sniper of some kind. A helicopter descends from nowhere belching fire. The sniper falls, blood blackening the asphalt. At night I emerge and obtain his rifle and ammunition. In the day I return to the ruin of the third floor with a few tins of 1950s pears and a supply of Corn Flakes and sit by a chink in the blasted wall, an opening screened by branches and recessed in the alley, with the dead man and a single bit of street perfectly encompassed by the scope. What better conditions to maximize the marksmanship of an amateur? Eventually, two more men arrive in an armored vehicle to attend to the body and my finger freezes as I'm taken by the thought that perhaps they too have a street somewhere and in confusion I fire, shattering the window of their vehicle. The dead man is removed. That night the retaliation is general. I'm thrown from bed and nearly blinded with debris as a shell blasts a hole through the second floor. I bundle the typewriter, food, papers and a little furniture down to the main floor which is bare, having been rented unfurnished to a group of students who had fled in the exodus. It was to that apartment we had moved from another house, the house where I was born. So long ago. It was a morning in the fall, I was about seven. We had only just settled in, the move had given me a little perspective and I took a walk around the block in a wild wind and there was a unity to everything, the houses, the trees, the sky, as if the block itself were separate, a world. Perhaps it was only the roar of the wind in my ears, for the sound has never quite gone away. I think I'd made it all a refuge, if only in the mind, from something terrible, something I'd wanted to get away from and now I'm there again as I sit on the sofa before the fireplace where I cook with burning rubbish and then continue work at the typewriter. At dusk I light candles and write, knowing the invasion will come at any moment. Or I walk the halls, pausing by a back room on the alley where I watched television much of the nine years that we were here, or simply stared. I excelled in art and a little physics, failed in everything else. My father looked at the art with interest moderated by skepticism, thought perhaps they had an idiot savant. He was a publicist and a connoisseur of painting and furniture, an impeccable dresser with a receding hairline and horn-rimmed glasses. He regarded me as a critic or a patron might regard a failed artist: with brisk, slightly sad resignation. He moved on. My mother, who looked a little like Beethoven – I mean the mane, the pug nose and the rumination – read all day or was distracted, found me fascinating only if viewed as a defective child out of Dickens or Dostoevsky, the only world she could stand sober. On her drunken binges she'd tell me I was the end of the line, the final outcome of some congenital dementia. Or she would refer to something terrible I had done, something unnamed of which I ought to have been aware. When I told her I couldn't remember she'd say I was lying and that whatever I had done was responsible for the slow destruction of the family, a moral problem, a Catholic problem, she herself guilty about being lapsed with the additional handicap of Irish descent. The apartment itself, with its inward-turning halls became a mental backwater of mortal sin introduced by the catechism and abetted by my mother. So I'd go upstairs and stay with my aunt and if the binge lasted, I'd be sent to stay with family friends in the area: for example, the Clemences along the street, the family that drove me up to school, the car filled with children, all sickly, neurasthenic, pale and unathletic, with allergies and phobias, pasty, pale and unsocial, their sole endowment a sort of affectless high intelligence, all of them raised on Wonder Bread and canned pork and beans, all knowing the

French Revolution by the age of eight, these the people with whom I was lucky enough to stay when my mother was convalescing. Finally, as I rode my scooter home on the day of the Cuban missile crisis, I watched for the attack, hoping the sky would ignite in a terminal conflagration destroying everything so that I wouldn't have arithmetic in the morning with Mrs. Carly who described to us how easily you could fall to hell and burn forever. There is a distant din now, perhaps engines or planes or tanks, as I wonder about the other side of the early '60s, the moderation of the climate when there was more fog, less heat, less destitution, less wealth, snow in winter, ball hockey over ice and broken concrete with my friend Stephen up the street; in spring, forsythia, lily of the valley, no one thought much about the climate, a quiet brilliance then, scarlet against grey, the overcast colour of sourceless light in early May, which may be part of the reason I can't leave, the immemorial relief of something horrible about to end. For example the academic year at the Catholic high school, a cesspit of ordained brutality, the home of all contempt and hatred, a stinking, terminal tidal flat of sin and corruption whence arose the final, fetid reek of the war, mass extermination and a bad conscience. One night at supper my mother told me about Mr. Spizarsky, a Pole who survived the Russians and the Nazis by lying for days among burned corpses. He rented a room a few doors up and used the prostitutes down by Roncesvalles. His fiancée had disappeared in the ruins of Europe before he cut his throat from loneliness in his top floor room. My mother told the story as if it were a warning; about what, I had no idea. My childhood ended abruptly in 1966 when I was diagnosed once and for all as defective and sent to a special class. My headaches increased, I ended up having surgery and lost my vital signs. In a few minutes I was brought back, my resuscitation marking an abrupt end to childhood which thenceforward subsisted only in memories that felt like someone else's. I emerged competent at obscure, specialized tasks. Reviling the past, I looked to the future. The child that I had once been now drifted like a speck in the evening sky, as if lodged in an event horizon, forever visible yet ungraspable. Which was why, in my early teens, I looked even more to far-off lands, like the next street over to the west and a rundown apartment block where Maxine and Marsha, two black sisters lived. Maxine was beautiful, three years older than I was and a daring extrovert; for a lark she got me into a night club where I sat uneasily, clumsy in my school blazer and tie and scuffed oxfords, and then she took me to their apartment where, with her, I lost my virginity. I later learned from her wise sister that she had done it to get her mind off a boyfriend. And then a few years later and again far to the west, an Italian girl around the corner whose name I don't recall, in another mock-Tudor house. We occasionally had sexual intercourse until she ended it at the insistence of her boyfriend. Such were my lessons in love before I was sent to France where I was finally free to develop a talent for obsessive fixation, sustained concentration on the minute and obscure and gained, very slowly, a career of carrying out mental tasks no one else wanted, such as collating historical data on happiness. In the same year, 1970, my parents bought the corner house, rented out the apartments and left for a peripatetic life between Europe and California; I hardly saw them again. The supersonic howl and thunder of fighter jets wakens me early; there follows a barrage, breaking all the windows. I pack up the manuscript, the typewriter and a suitcase and head north, passing the other rental property just up the street. I decide to check on the tenant but when I knock the door drifts open. The house has been looted, the poor old woman having fled, leaving a spattering of blood in dust in empty rooms. I have not seen these rooms in fifty-odd years. I ascend the stairs, past the empty spaces that had been a hall, a bedroom, a library. Above me, on the third floor is, or perhaps, a spare room I had loved and which I used to pretend was my office, a place where I imagined I'd work all my life. I wonder if it's still the same. It was from this house that two little girls, sisters, from across the street, took me two doors up to Mr. Spizarsky's where he drunkenly showed us newspaper photographs of torture victims of the Nazis. Around the same time, the street emptied as the families moved to the suburbs. It was then that everything began to end, ended for good when I was sent to the first day of kindergarten with the Clemences, up the hill to the Convent School and the suffocating smell of baking, steam pipes, fingerpaint and the sound of a piano and of a bell ringing for the children to sit down. They were short a chair and I was still on my feet and the nun was enraged. She seized me and beat me in the head, slamming me into the floor in front of the class until I was thrown into the girls' washroom with paper towel to stop the bleeding. I was examined and my parents said things I never quite understood about a head injury and about the nun being a poor soul but that something ought to be done about her. I had problems perceiving and reading. My mother had already begun to drink; downstairs in the dining room in heavy evening light she'd sit while I ate my supper and tell me of the terrible problems I had caused for the family and that the Chinese had a bomb that would reduce us all to ashes. The northeast bedroom is mostly unchanged. As a child I had imagined I would live forever in the house of my birth, that there would be no history. There had been no sense of change then, only the instinctive apprehension of eternal forms and shapes in chairs, tables, lamps, the sky, the ideal images in children which die with duration, change, decay. Draining away from the time in the garden at the back when I'd played with my best friend Stephen, frail, blond and cerebral. We invented mythologies about the streets and the block, we dug holes in the yard, holes that we thought would get us through to China. It's much the same, the house, the backyard where I'd played with the little girls across the street before everything happened. I think I was three, the sisters were two or three years older. The sisters who had introduced me to the world beyond, gave me the courage to go all the way west to Christie Pits Park where there had been grandeur and crowds under vast, lowering evening skies, the sisters who took me to the grocery store at closing where they shoplifted, who towed me around in my wagon in the backyard under the wondrous skies of fire in the west where I believed far lands and the future lay, the yard where the children of the street, the girls in their white socks played to the sound of the passing train; where I saw the first sun, sky, moon and snowfall and the first faraway girls, where I saw Bev, the intoxicating smell of the earth in spring. And Wendy, the younger of the two sisters across the street, Wendy whom I found again, loved and buried. And now I do not hear the train. The fighting encroaches from north and south, getting louder and closer as I wonder about the relentlessness of time and then the room, the grass, the sky, where it all might have stopped and stayed and not gone onward.

AFTER HISTORY –BUT NOT LAST

Parts of the city were still crowded with wires and poles in late sun, bits of broken cornice on shopfronts crested with filthy ornament, blackened armorial bearings in sandstone, bird shit. On the evening I'd driven in I suddenly realized I had nowhere to stay, so I parked the car and checked into the first hotel I saw. The room was cheap with a high ceiling; early evening light in an old sash window covered in dust. My few possessions sat on the bed. I dressed in a dark suit and went out for a walk. I'd grown up here, I'd been away I don't know how long. But everything had changed. It was crisper and cleaner with an empty efficiency, the skies clearer; there was less in the air, no longer the haze or the stained sunsets, the dirge of foghorns. There were straight lines now, windowless structures without visible function. And then in the morning, the prospect of the job, of expenses. I didn't want to die, but I hadn't the least desire to move forward. It's true I'd become a drunk, but consider for a moment the intensity, the night-fire feeling of alcohol, the violent swimming, the turbulence, the headlong moving, the floating streets, the grandeur, the music, the strangeness of the sky, the legions, leopard skin on crested brass helmets, the terror in tails of flying horsehair, faint yellow in dark light as if in a painted picture in a dark dream of massed columns. I'd been eased out of the university in the city from which I had driven. They had anticipated resistance, indignation, had offered me probation, a defence of my place on the tenure track, I'd been put there by someone long ago, a body, a committee, I don't remember, I'd had allies, most of them unwanted, people had used words like systemic and political in my defence, I was offered rehabilitation. It was true I had stumbled and fallen down a lot, said things I shouldn't have, missed classes. I had never wanted tenure or even the rank of professor, had never wanted to do research or to publish, had never wanted to join organizations, boards, committees, had only wanted to lecture. I liked giving lectures. My lectures had been popular; they were very dramatic, even, perhaps especially, when I was drunk. When I left, there was a lot of handshaking and wishing me well. As if they felt guilty. In the city of my birth, a lecturer in European history had died suddenly in mid-term. How, otherwise, would I have found work as a lecturer, at this university, in European History? Still, having failed to become a responsible member of a community, I would have to try again, making the world a better place, giving of oneself as someone had said, giving back, making a difference, all in all good elegy and eulogy material. Which is why I did not want to leave the room, the hotel room. I was also afraid of my reception at home, for I still knew people. The street on which I had grown up was intact, I was pretty sure my mother was still alive, the street of two solid blocks, the houses, alleys, yards where I still had friends, old and young, tenants, neighbours, the houses red brick, distinguished by a variety of dormers and verandas, sandstone lintels, the sound of children, the great elms and maples, my uncle who had the second floor of the corner house, my aunt on the top floor calling her cat, the yellow fire of forsythia in faint mist at the ends of the streets and the brass chorus, the green, the red piping, the molded fire-stricken masses on horseback under a roiling sky of thunder, the dark columns moving over the face of the earth with flags and smoke, the toy soldiers, Nutcracker wars, frogging and white cross-belts, headdresses, the images impossible, a legend, unreal. I'd been taken to Paris when I was thirteen and we were in Les Invalides, could not quite distinguish what it was above me, something dark, faded, red, white and blue curtains of flags, the actual flags of Jena and Austerlitz, Friedland from improbable paintings, the flags hung close together, serried, rotting in the roof of the choir, evidence that it had not been made up, the only true evidence of the past, any past, no longer magic but real and ancient yet present. I was still in the hotel room, I got up off the bed, found my way to the university. I was introduced to other faculty members, graduate students. Without a drink. They all drank. They had coolers and martinis. Various studies, subaltern studies, doctorates on comic strips and transgression. Since I hadn't the wit or the will to alter the evaluations from the previous institution, I was more or less on probation at this one. I smiled quickly when encountering other staff members, went home in the evening, left the hotel early to arrive at my lectures punctually, most of them on Napoleonic Europe, the Confederation of the Rhine, negotiations over the Grand Duchy of Warsaw, the imperial policy

of the Austrian empire, Franco-Turkic relations etcetera, it was
my specialty but something was missing even though I drama-
tized it, exhorted, expatiated, veered into wild, sarcastic fugues
about the rule of Murat as King of Rome, could not hear myself
for the laughter and applause, didn't know what it meant,
didn't care. I was worried about ending up on the street, so
great was the impending threat of a return to alcoholism, I saw
myself begging, searching through trash containers, so I
attended every faculty meeting; since the department was on
the left I signed petitions, wrote about corporate responsibility
in the department newsletter, fought to defend female engi-
neering students. But it wasn't just about being removed again;
the threat was more general, invisible, it was in the air between
Carruthers Hall and the shawarma place filled with noisy tech
school students with caps on sideways and low-hanging
pants, the only place I was sure I'd meet no one from the university. The pressures of the department followed me about
as much as the other thing loomed ahead, waited. I did not
know what it was; sometimes it seemed like a tidal wave as
high as the houses, a wall of approaching darkness, a mon-
strous scorched face with a burning mouth. As I passed them,
the staff members maintained a posture of distant neutrality.
There was one woman I was attracted to, I kept meeting her at
dinners and events, I listened carefully, tried to acquaint myself
with her and her friends and colleagues and get the lay of the
land but the fact remained: I had not done drugs, had not been
married, separated or divorced, was not gay, did not have children, had never paid support, had never contemplated the burden of being male, had never thought much about my gender,

had never been a promiscuous or cantankerous older man, did not play squash or go to the gym, did not have affairs with younger women or other people's wives, had never been called a sexist, had never slept with a feminist, did not compete for honours or recognition, had never tried to conquer the world with my book, I had no book. Nor was I engaged with a world defined by ethnicity and freedom, the free market, liberty, architectural masterpieces in amazing new materials, events, universities and art galleries with CEOs, the biology of the brain, the frontiers of neuroscience, the existence or nonexistence of God, the benefits or the horrors of religion or the sacred. I only wanted to go home, the old street, the faces, but I had fallen out of touch. Which was why I held on to the hotel room, a place requiring neither decision nor commitment and reflecting nothing of me, and where nothing intruded; perhaps for that very reason it felt like my own. I'd been offered a small apartment in residence by the dean. She'd made a friendly comic gesture to show I had her attention, you could tell she had no idea who she was talking to, as I found with an increasing number of people; you could see at parties and events, the speedy tact with which they moved on to the next person; that's not to say they were not inclusive, they had hired a dwarf computer technician, had called a meeting about an ugly girl who'd been raped and nearly drowned during frosh week, a victim of hazing by both sexes. There was talk of misogyny, regulations, measures taken or not taken; the words remiss, horrific and abhorrent were used repeatedly but the word cruelty was never used, not once. I have little memory of childhood, but there had always been a shadow of cruelty, I'd been subjected to it now and then. I hated cruelty, it made me violent. Back in the hotel room I felt something dark beyond the walls, wanted to move out but didn't know where. It was late November when I walked up to the old street, knocked at a big old house, the ground-floor apartment where I'd lived with my parents, a woman answered; she'd never heard of them, the tenants before her had been Croatian. My aunt and uncle were long gone; a second-floor tenant had heard my uncle had died years after he'd moved out. I inquired elsewhere on the block, all the others had died or were gone, there were no addresses, no contact numbers. The street was clean with a dust of crumbled leaves. The houses were the same, several had had their bricks washed, but otherwise the same, astoundingly, nothing altered, the trees the same as if everything had fallen unconscious, the gutters, the sewer gratings, the phone posts, the alleys reverberating with footsteps, that springing sound between the walls, close bay windows in driveways like passages in a medina, the gables, the sandstone faces and leopards, the carved verandas and pillars, a minor Carthage of temple porches built by Dido, the shafts of sun in yards, the stirring of bare branches in a faint breeze, the sun at evening. The street lights came on. The absence in the street; prior to the absence, perhaps some part of myself had been there, and I'd thought I could recover it, live in it but it was absent. I stood in the hotel room, streetlights on, still like the sad white gems I'd seen as I'd walked home from school in winter. The window, the lights, taillights and distant neon, logos, ferocious lightning communication, transmission of thoughts, to what end, what improvement, cheaper, faster, cleaner, an ideal of quantity, the onrush of electrons, what was the conviction, efficiency, rationality, equity, was there any reason to think that the plan of a city or a temple did not still reflect the plan of the cosmos, surely it hadn't been proven wrong so much as forgotten, I wanted to get a drink, stopped myself. In the staff lounge I took a drink when no one was around, the dead hour of four. Between lectures, I went back to the street, in the silence an echo in nothing and a sparrow flew past as if through a ruin. In the afternoon as the first snow fell only the ceiling of cloud moved, the trees bare against the dying sky. But there was still the train, the train still passed up at the end of the street, the whisper-roar diminishing, I had tried and failed to write a play to that sound, upstairs, in a front room, a large dark window, young, grizzled, in an old black suit with a vest, intoxicated by the wet black trees of March, a dull sun in a dun-coloured sky, the last of the heavy wet snow speckled with grime, receding ice and running water, the eaves dripping, the sounds of pigeons in the eaves, there had been something even then, something that would still not disclose itself. And now the silence, as if everyone had died and then back in the hotel the sense of retribution, the approaching wave, Leviathan, the Ouroboros, its eyes burning mad with blood in the night, breathing the pulse of the times. It was still there when I wakened. The department head, her neutral attention, students perhaps feeling they had been cheated because I'd been drunk when I'd given the lecture on Catherine the Great's revival of the Zemstvos but I had told them: what ferment, what intoxication, a Russian monarch moved by the streets of Paris two thousand miles away to resurrect some ancient peasant autonomy etcetera. I became lost in it, I was going to be gotten rid of, it would be even easier than last time, I was placed on probation, I had little job security, my heart was elsewhere, I felt it very strongly, I was not imagining it. There was a furnished apartment for rent in the corner house on the old street, a former mansion broken up, four-square, blackened sandstone and brick, rather high, slate roofs, wide dormers, immense chimneys. I had known that house; now four apartments had been put in on the ground floor. I took the one on the east side, it had a large room with large windows looking east on the dying leaves and the crabbed bass tree and the old street; the bedroom faced onto the alley that adjoined the neighbouring house. Daily, I left the apartment, did my lectures, came back. I regained the peace I'd had in the hotel. The world receded a little, technology, the global economy, the destruction of nature, small wars, isolated catastrophes as on the eve of World War One, efficiency, innovation, all of it sleepwalking. The main room hadn't been repainted, had remained grey all those years, I sat on the sofa a long time until I saw that everything was gone. I kept going to work, the world of convenience, practicality, wires, connections, the positivist, small job world where everything had slowed to bits, bytes, an attenuated, dreary, perpetual present. Yet always the wall, the advancing wave of the upended grave, the darkness. When I was asleep it was still there but instead of ahead it was under the floor; in the daytime it had retreated to the northeast corner of the room, dark and penetrating like a liquid and one evening it oozed out as a war, the first to shine through in the reversed shadows of the glass plate negative, only fifty years after Waterloo, photons coalescing into the heavy grey forms of the eye-rolled dead of Antietam, the utter, shabby truth of eternal destruction within memory of the cross-belted toy soldier wars, the unreal real, torn to shreds, cloth, cartridge paper, stained rags, litter blown off falling bodies, rolled and stale in trampled darkened black and white grass, bloated half-bearded faces, the odour seeping through in photons onto the book page. Another time voices, many voices, crowds, a surge of lung power, phalanxes, wakening to the tram wires and surging masses, St. Petersburg. Russia, the USSR, overwhelming national effort, the eternal in the palm of the hand, forward in word and deed, visions of life, of a way to live, the flags, the fire, the stars, the star on the Kremlin, the bookshelf, the grey room, yes, my living room, my parents' bedroom where I'd been conceived, we'd had the ground floor then, now it was four units with smudged and battered white doors with black numbers. The early '6os, the air had been gentle with more mist, the climate cooler then, forsythia, lily of the valley, news of nations in static on radios, my uncle upstairs had often talked about 1917, parades, ideas galvanized with material force, a fascination, a feeling for life, a better life for friends, neighbours, unions, parades, belief, factories, fire, messages in the sky in vapor trails in the blood of sunset, distant vast music, the masses and the factories on the street that ran by the tracks, hydro poles into the conflagration of sunset, the tracks where I still heard the train, breathing in the night, the wailing horn of half a century before, legions in industry, baroque factories like castle keeps over neighbourhood roofs, lanes, yards, streets, generations of machinists, food and metal workers, lunch pails in fog that carried the factory whistle, the Nazis, five hundred shining helmets gliding like a single oiled machine, the red, black and white swastika banners in the wind, massive columns of history, monolithic, the cesspit, the oozing charnel house, such stunning grandeur for an idea as small and impoverished as one man's solitary, drunken, weeping rant at night in front of the mirror. But before the truncated, aborted grandeur, before the deception, something behind the columns, a darkening temple porch larger than man rooted in legend and myth, yes, belief. What had been the seed, what had it come from, the crowds, the weeping, the waving, the waiting? The apartment had backed onto that same alley, I had the same bedroom, the same window lit only by a strip of broken sky, I remembered you could fall into the abyss of the alley if you didn't reach, leap in your sleep across to the neighbouring house, hold on to the yards and gardens, kitchens, halls and bedrooms, the people talking at night before it emptied into a sea of privation, of silence. I got drunk again, this time with acquaintances in a bar near the university. I forget its name, blond, yellow, library wood, bloodless, minimal. The ephemeral, the desultory, the insolent and tribalized, an economy evolved haphazardly into something unknown and autonomous, not even a nightmare but an endless nervous banality, small ideas, small careers, unfinished, short term, transient, convenient, streets without meaning, avenues without aspect, vistas of clutter, life as a self-serve buffet, the world of the personal, the chorus of history reduced to a few theme songs, an end to history in balance sheets. The sepulchre of the street, the ash skies of old Advent, dead memory of the song of cardinals in spring, leaves clattering down an alley, the hollow roar of the wind in the trees, the rattle of glass. Something like the distant trumpet of an angel sounded and was gone. I'd gained some time by agreeing to lecture on the history of the North Atlantic cod fishery. There was a family I'd known a few blocks over, I rang their bell, they were still there, heavy, aged, weary, soft, devoid of affect, said we have something of yours and handed me a box of books, I recognized the worn spines, titles and covers that no longer blinded, no longer consumed like a narcotic. What had been in the corner of the room was a bookshelf, the line of cavalry, not figures in a picture but men remembered, mounted, heaving headlong, flung toward a ditch, the white vectors of swords, flying sabretaches, breastplates dull in the gunpowder occluded sun, horsehair flying like thoughts of Satan from Spartan helmets across the ditch, the abyss, the sunken road to Louvain, revealed like a break of light, witnessed by the dead, the will, the idea, a single front of a thousand horsemen, cuirassiers, horse grenadiers, serried, crushed, crammed, lifted, lancers, chasseurs, dragoons, burnished in dying sun, empress green, the glorious insanity, white lapel fronts spattered, brass buttons, imperial saddles, slashed, epaulettes, headless bodies riding a few yards yet, lanyards flying in the smoking air, unburdened by morality, the receding stained mirrors of liberty, equality, fraternity, republic, nation, empire barely sustained in a straining leap, the dried mud, the temperature that day, the books in the bookshelf, blind force of imagination and love beyond practical well-being, equal citizens waiting in equal houses for something in the sky, towering above common or garden reason and fear of death, there has to be something more than justice, more than the greed of the rich and the poor and the comfortable, more than the vanity of altruism, the Old Guard on review, glorious beyond rationality, the white, the blue, the bearskin, the red, the gold, the chalked belts, the man in plain green and a grey coat, as simple as will, simple as an idea, cocked hat and ranks of piping and epaulettes, women mourning and ecstatic in empire dresses, the fallen conscripts of 1813, smoke as high as cumulus over fields and cypress, cities, spires, lines of regiments remote as a bird call. What if there had never been any striving to leap, any pillared porches of Carthage where everyone talks into the night, any Waterloo, struggle, greatcoats; no great hammer and sickle, no glory, no dead, no Marx or the ineffable in clouds of eagles? Nothing ever like glory, not even from books or the words of the dead, or even in failure on St. Helena, even in the hypocrisy and the grubbing for honours, the more progress, the more progress is murdered; the more peace, the more anomie; the more despair, the vaster the plain of smallness, of ennui. I quit the university. I now wait for the money to run out in the inexpressible silence of Les Invalides and sleep forever in the voices, the sound of distant crowds rather than waken; even the blind will in darkness is better than times without affect or aspect which eddy and merge into a plain without hope or end, this faint horizon and listless wind.

LAST

Henry Last answered an ad for accommodation in a country house in the centre of France. It was a small, provincial villa and Last's room had long glass doors out onto rolling plains of wheat and barley. Here, finally, was a place that was tolerable. As long as people remained at arm's length. Above all, Last avoided close relationships. To his advantage his appearance was such as to excite very little interest. Once nearly handsome, he now had greying brown hair, gold-rimmed glasses and a slight paunch. He was often a day unshaven and always wore a blazer as if to discourage any suggestion of activity. Last was fifty years old.

That night, he sat at the window and watched the fall of dusk. Over the following days he had his breakfast and lunch in the village and the maid gave him his supper in the kitchen. The rest of the time he read and kept notes and a diary. In the evening he would walk in the lanes that ran over the grain fields and smoke a single cigarette. He kept clear of the couple that owned the farm, the elder daughter and two unnerving, horrible adolescent children who came on weekends.

But minimal contact became unavoidable, for there were only two ways out of the house – through the kitchen, which was usually occupied, and through the front door. Next to the front door was the farm office where Morand, the proprietor, was usually on the telephone or doing accounts. He turned out to be a hydraulic engineer who worked on irrigation projects in North Africa and for half the year lived at the farm to manage the grain crop and its harvest. He had the cigarette-thickened voice of the old chanteurs, a rugged tan and black eyes. About the third time that Last approached the door on his way to the village, Morand asked if everything were all right and they chatted about literature.

Last regretted this because he was soon invited to dinner. He tried to find a way out but in the end acceptance seemed less of a statement. The invitation became weekly. Throughout, he was almost always silent.

One evening, hardly anyone else spoke either. The tension was evident in the slim, rigid posture of Madame Morand, at once balletic and imperious, suggesting diets, pills, surgical tucks, and also in the nervous flinch under one eye. There were reasons for this. The farm was in her family and her husband managed it. But the real focus of her husband's life was the period of his yearly absence in the Maghreb, while Madame's focus was him. The odd time that Last had been directed to an upstairs bathroom he saw that Morand slept in an unmade single bed in a storage room and there was usually a book about the Third Reich or the Resistance pages opened on a chair that served as a night table. Meanwhile, Madame slept in a large Louis XVI bed in a big, commodious, bright bedroom. Presumably there was the problem of a mistress.

The couple spent their days apart. Only at lunch and dinner did they face one another. On this particular evening, the silence was broken by the excruciating banging of a dessert spoon on a glass by Nadine, Madame's twenty-year-old daughter from a previous marriage to a Moroccan airline pilot. Nadine was dark, intellectually quick, voluptuous and lazy. Across from her and beside Last sat the adolescent daughter and son who arrived on weekends from summer studies in Paris, the horrible children Last disliked. They were loud, confident and prim, students in business administration. Nadine, too, despised them.

But Nadine's precociousness and egocentricity also irritated Last. When her stepfather occasionally recited Mallarmé, she corrected it. She spoke passionately about various authors, sometimes on the verge of tears, saying to anyone, save Last, who stayed well clear, "But you don't understand! You don't feel it!" She also laughed loud and hard like a man. She and her mother occasionally had vicious fights concerning Nadine's impatience and rudeness about life in the country. Nadine was more affectionate with her stepfather. But during her attempted chats with him in his office, he would drift back to his long-distance calls and Nadine would leave quietly. Morand hadn't much time for her. At best, his half-Arab stepdaughter bewitched, amused him, much as he was fascinated by the aquifers of the Maghreb. Her mother, meanwhile, was so preoccupied by her husband's complacency and cheerful evasion of marital responsibility that she hadn't much time for Nadine either. The silence at the table continued until Madame hurled down her napkin, upsetting her glass and left the table, slamming the glass door.

Perhaps it was due to their inability to deal with one another that the family seemed to like Last. Certainly, Last himself could see no other reason. The next night that Last was present at dinner Morand extended a hand toward him and remarked, as if to surprise everyone, *"Il connait bien son Baudelaire."* Last shifted uncomfortably. After dinner at coffee in the drawing room, Nadine asked him to look at an essay she had written for a remedial course earlier that summer. She was enrolled at the Sorbonne but due to a disinclination to work and popularity with the male students she had failed French Literature. She handed him the paper. It was about Baudelaire. Last did not want to do this but couldn't see any way out; he was living there.

He read it that evening. She had talent, wit and her own voice; there was no doubt. It occurred to him that she would go farther than he had. But she was confused about the poet's dislike of nature. She had romanticized Baudelaire; his life was more tedious than his mystique suggested and ennui understood as boredom and emptiness rather than as longing was necessary to understanding his poetry. They discussed it later that evening. To Last's surprise, she responded to these observations with chastened silence.

This, however, did not have the effect for which he had hoped. Despite all efforts to plot his movements in and out of the house with the end of avoiding the others, he kept encountering Nadine in the front foyer through which it was impossible not to pass. She lounged in an armchair and read magazines or made long-distance telephone calls to the few friends in Paris who hadn't left for the summer. Once, she cut her call short to ask him about Malcom Lowry. Another time she was about to dial when she asked him about the weather. And so on. He would be brusque, barely polite, raise his hand and move off.

The following day, which was humid and exhausting, Last looked forward to his after-dinner cigarette more than ever. The weather was grey, the air still. The rye was fragrant as he lit up and pulled the smoke deep into his lungs. He had been there two months and to his surprise he was not tired of it. He was thinking that here, finally, was one place he never wanted to leave when he saw Nadine approaching. She'd been sunbathing and had pulled on her shorts and top over her bathing suit. She asked if she could join him; he assented without enthusiasm. They chatted about her previous year at the Sorbonne, Last volunteering as little as possible. It was in her French Literature class that she had finally found love; she had fallen for her literature professor. He was estranged from his wife but as soon as Nadine moved in with him he became as possessive, silly and jealous as a teenager. She left him in disgust and her work slackened even more. She had spent all her money on clothes and parties and that was why her stepfather had grounded her out in the country for the summer. She decided she had never really been in love and now she was trapped here, bored to death and convinced that her parents didn't love her either.

"Why did you like the literature professor?" Last asked.

"Because he was intelligent and accomplished. And he was serious; he didn't have his tongue hanging out after women all the time. I guess it was because he didn't seem to care. He was so cool. It was a challenge. And then, of course, he turned out to be like everyone else. An idiot. You'd think that men would be more different from each other the better you got to know them, but they turn out to be even more the same."

Last had no response. After a considerable silence she said, "I guess I'm depressed about my stepfather... I really like him and he treats me well and all but I don't think he really loves me."

Last had come to wonder if such a thing as love existed and so he mused reluctantly that stepparents and children had to know one another as individuals first. Beyond that, what was love? We didn't really know whether we meant devotion, instinct, fascination, attraction, duty and so on.

"You mean maybe there's not such a thing as love?" she said.

"Maybe."

Nadine seemed to take some encouragement from this and went on to talk about her childhood. In Rabat, Morocco, where she had grown up with Madame Morand, her original father spent much of his time with his mistress in Casablanca. The rest of the time he was flying 747s or staying with mistresses in different capitals. During vacations and holidays he would stop by the family and play the impresario, showering them with gifts and then disappear again. Her mother despised him. As Nadine grew up Madame tried to exert her own frustrated authority over her daughter and finally became controlling. After they moved to Paris, and Nadine was in *lycée*, the boys who pursued her all seemed like her father –

empty, sex-crazed idiots. They walked on and he felt her put her arm through his.

That night, Last lay in bed waiting for sleep to come. It had been his distant, dimly recalled experience that women imposed themselves on men only when the attraction was too strong to resist and sooner or later it always became physical. But the prospect of hurting Nadine seemed just as bad: for that too would be a form of entanglement. Every day, after all, he looked forward to nothing more than sleep; sometimes he looked forward to it all day. Above all he wanted peace, even entropy. This, in fact, was the plan for what remained of his life. He wanted solitude and if Nadine began to pay too much attention to him he would simply tell her about his past. Then, surely, she'd be more than happy to leave him alone.

One night at dinner, Last noticed her staring at him. A couple of times the following day he sensed that she wanted to talk to him and seemed hurt by his brusque, if polite, avoidance.

The following Saturday the family had planned a long drive to Tours to join friends for dinner in a restaurant. Last was invited and went along only because he had read about Tours and couldn't be bothered to go and see it on the bus. The teenagers were down from Paris and there was not enough room in Madame Morand's Peugeot. As a consequence, the hired man agreed to drive Nadine and her half-sister in the old Deux Chevaux. Last had tried to ride with the parents but somehow the only space left was in the Deux Chevaux, in the back seat with Nadine. He was at a complete loss as to how this had happened.

The dinner in Tours was a great bore. He could find no opportunity to leave and see the city. The Morands' friends were even more constrained than the Morands themselves by the latest trends and fads of the upper middle-class. The younger people, with whom the Paris teenagers fell in right away, were nondescript and fascinated with computers to the exclusion of anything else and all their references were to things American. It had been a long time, anyway, since Last had made conversation with strangers. Everything served to reinforce his total indifference and he remained mostly silent and immobile. Nadine socialized. Eventually he noticed her watching him from various points in the restaurant. Even while dancing. It seemed it was time to tell her the story.

For a while, the drive back in the Deux Chevaux was silent. Then Nadine asked Last what he thought about the dinner. He managed a polite evasion. The country outside passed in darkness. His hand was on the seat, her little finger on top of his. He knew that neither the hired man nor her half-sister Cecile, who was in the front seat, spoke English fluently. Also, the engine of the Deux Chevaux was very loud inside the car. He shifted his hand away and in English, told Nadine the story of his life.

Last had been raised in Toronto by highly literate parents, neither of whom had fulfilled their aspirations. This led them to the mistake of placing all their hopes in Last. It was when he was eighteen, during a year abroad at school in Lyon, France, that he had felt a mission to write poetry. To pay his way, after university, Last started a column with poetry reviews in a major Toronto newspaper and its success attracted the woman, an investigative journalist, who became his wife. During the first years of their marriage, however, he reverted to the actual writing of poetry, wrestling anew with persistent images. Out of this Last produced a single poem which can only be summarized as an image of vast greyness upon which there is a point of vermilion which brightens and fades, and it was considered brilliant and published widely. As he pursued his poetry, the column began to flag; his wife warned him of this and they fought about it.

"What she had the acuity to see, long before I did," Last explained to Nadine in the darkness, over the drone of the engine, "was that I really didn't have any talent. I was a one-shot wonder."

His wife then had two stillbirths and they were advised not to try again to have children. Last strove to meet the expectations of his first poem until his column, increasingly neglected, deteriorated rapidly and was discontinued. When his wife left him he was broken and he dulled himself with an avalanche of meaningless freelance work. By the time that he had taken the poetry in hand again, he had grown apart from his friends and from his wife who had become famous and successful.

It was on a spring day that he actually saw one of the images that had moved him so: a dull sun shining through a dirty sky. The image still spoke to him but he didn't know what it meant. It was then that he realized he had no talent. He had sacrificed his life to an illusion. He also realized, in retrospect, that everyone else had known it all along. When he'd imagine their two children who had died near birth, he'd break down. He'd collapse. He was forty-seven.

"The worst was still to come," he now said to Nadine. He glanced at her but in the dark splashed with patches of passing light he could not quite see her.

"With nowhere to turn, I finally did the things we are supposed to do. I acknowledged my failings and built up hope and courage. I fell in love with my ex-wife all over again and tried to get her back but she wasn't interested. Anyway, it turned out she was seeing someone else. But she and her boyfriend were kind. They introduced me to some single women friends, but in the end none of them were really interested. Gradually I became withdrawn. I saw a psychiatrist for a year but nothing transpired. I did yoga for a while and transcendental meditation, but the fact was those things do not make up for having no mooring in life, no money, no friends. Then I got a life-threatening case of pneumonia and went into the hospital for two months. A couple of people were aware of it but no one came to see me. When I got out I attempted suicide with barbiturates and was found because the landlord made an impromptu showing of the apartment. It occurred to me then that one could live and die another way by detaching oneself from people and allowing the end to come on its own; to live without will, without talent, without aspirations. So I withdrew my savings and decided to live in France. I'd lived there before, in Lyon, as a student. But I no longer knew anyone there and was confident I wouldn't be recognized or contacted. Having nothing to contribute to the world, the best I can do is pay my way and I've decided to live for the duration of the money. I wanted to live alone in the middle of the countryside, but I could only afford to rent a room in a house. So that's how I ended up here."

He looked at her warily. Nadine seemed to frown in a sort of confusion. Then she said, "You've lived through death." Last drifted off and slept for much of the way back. He loved sleep.

Now, when Last went out for his after-dinner smoke, he was sure he'd be left alone. It was only the threat of rain clouds that caused him to look back and notice Nadine approaching.

"I was thinking about what you told me in the car," she said. Last listened as she went on about her family. They passed over a crest in a field of oats. "And so," she said, "because my father wasn't there, the psychiatrist told me I have an idealized image of men which no man can equal. What I want is the impossible. Someone intelligent, handsome, strong, sensitive, talented, honest and decisive with a sense of humour. Or at least most of those." The crickets throbbed in the grey heat. She was walking close to him.

Though he scarcely looked at her, he was aware of her sensuality. It was just there; relentlessly, indeed remorselessly, it imposed itself despite all of Last's feelings about life or the world. In fact, to his disappointment, he had an erection. They approached a large shallow valley where a stream ran. He was baffled; it wouldn't go down. She sat on the crest of land and looked up at him, her eyes pausing briefly on his aroused state. He sat down quickly and avoided saying anything. After a silence, she said, "Nobody ever told me about themselves the way you did." The land shimmered in twilight. The grain fields leaned into the torn sky of dusk.

"What a sky," she said.

"It's actually pollution," he said. "In fact, urban pollution makes the colours even stronger. It's the only thing I miss about

the city." He fell silent. There was nothing more to say. He
didn't want to get up too abruptly and he didn't want to hurt
her. Yet he couldn't stand the silence. "Sunsets are essentially
dirt," he said. "People don't realize that. The more dust, sul-
phides and carbon monoxide, the more colour."

She burst out laughing and thrust her fist into the air. They
walked back in silence. Effortlessly, she took his hand. He let it
hang there indifferently then released it as gently as he could
when they approached the house.

A couple of days later, notes he was making on Nietzsche
began, for the first time, to apply to Blake. The connections, it
would later turn out, were vague if not completely spurious but
he was absorbed and happy. That night, he dozed off con-
tented and exhausted. Vaguely, he heard a sort of rattle but
turned over and slept again. There was a word like those you
hear uttered on the edge of consciousness. He opened his
eyes. Nadine wore an old navy blue bathrobe. She softly closed
the door. He asked her what she wanted. She lowered her
eyes, then sat down on the bed with a sort of unhappy deci-
siveness.

"What's the problem?" he asked.

"Nothing," she said.

"I'm trying to sleep. It's three in the morning."

She sat facing away from him for an interval then sank awkwardly, half sideways, falling on his chest. Her hair was flaxen,
fragrant.

At this moment, Last's mind was blank. He stroked her
thick tresses listlessly. Then he stopped and waited, hoping she
would leave.

"Do you really think this is right?" he said. But the chant of the crickets through the window seemed to make them untouchable. "I don't think you really know what you're doing," he continued. "You probably think you're very much of the world but you have no idea how young you are." His words trailed off weakly. As she sighed he felt her bosom rise and fall and then felt an alien tenderness. She moved her lips past the top of the sheet and kissed his chest. He tried to lie still. He sighed and lightly took the collar of the dressing gown, held it for a while, then haltingly pushed it down over her shoulders. She slid a knee up on the bed, slipped one arm out of the dressing gown and then the other. Her body was full but nowhere fat. Her breasts seemed swollen. It had been a lifetime since he had been with a young woman. She shifted and her nipples brushed across him; they were hard. She slid down into the bed beside him and began to kiss him.

He thought of forcing her out but even if it were only the maid who was wakened, it would end everything; the old woman had a habit of casually commenting to Madame on the movements of everyone she heard and saw, no matter how banal. He tried to get his mind on something else but she was scissoring his thigh between her own and pushing her vulva against him. Helplessly, he slid his hand down her stomach; he was surprised by the enthusiasm of her clitoris. In a pathetic bid for some sort of control he tried to see if he could produce pleasure without producing any passion, if such a thing was possible. Out of practice, out of shape, he was slow. It turned out, to his confusion, that this was what she liked; part of the problem, no doubt, with all those young men. The remaining concern was that they not waken the others in the house. Painfully, Last kept trying to hold her still, listening until he found a way that produced no creak in the bed. This discovery had the opposite effect; in the end, he had to put his hand over her mouth. She slept on top of him a while, one knee drawn up, then left him. Last was utterly wasted.

In mid-morning, with a feeling of guilt, Last had coffee with M. Morand and they chatted about agricultural practises sixty years before. As recently as the war, forty men and three teams of horses had been needed to bring the harvest. He loved the image and began to wonder how he could ensure his stay there. Fortunately, Nadine would return to Paris in September but it was still early August and he worried that if she became upset with him, her parents might catch on. That day, to his relief, he saw little of her; she was on errands in the town with her mother.

During Last's final dinner with the family everything was normal: Nadine had a fight with her mother and her stepfather rolled his eyes. Then, Madame Morand turned to Last: "Michel is going to Tunisia in September. He and my sister don't get along and her husband just died." She paused, uncertain how to proceed.

"I think I understand...You need the room," Last said, trying to be sporting.

"I'm sorry, but there's no other way. We hope you can come back next summer."

He improvised quickly to save them any guilt or embarrassment: "I'd wanted to spend some time in Lyon anyway. I went to school there, I wouldn't mind seeing how it's changed." But he had a sudden feeling of panic, of sadness.

At three in the morning as Last lay awake, the chant of the crickets in the darkness brought close the recollection of Nadine. The unexpected end had filled him with desire. He could not believe he missed her and he resisted the feelings all the more resolutely. The remaining days were a struggle. He managed to convey some affection and keep his distance at the same time. Nadine was inscrutable; as self-possessed as on the day he had met her. He contemplated the future. Once again he faced insecurity and nothingness. Having no idea where he would go, he decided, finally, on Lyon; at least he knew it.

On the train through the strange sterility of the Massif Central, he reflected on their last kiss at the train station. Morand had been nearby and it was the simple *baiser* on both cheeks but he thought he had detected a certain warmth. On repeated reflection, he reassured himself that she loved him.

Over the next two weeks fear, alienation and confusion pushed every trace of Nadine from his mind. His lack of purpose stared him in the face and the city was no longer the Lyon of his youth. It had a subway now; Rue Victor Hugo had been turned into a pedestrian mall; some high-rises had gone up in Villeurbanne. Barely, however, and with difficulty, he got used to it. It was true that it had lost some of its misty grubbiness but, as it turned out, none of the mythical quality for which he remembered it: the *centre-ville* was still dimly lit with points of neon just as he had seen it long ago at night when he was drunk; the nooks and crannies, the dark bars. The prostitutes were still in the same streets; here, at least, was continuity.

There were even intense, moving memories; particularly of a streetwalker gently washing his penis in a sink. The firm understanding of her grasp.

It was on Rue Victor Hugo that he got a fifth-floor flat: a large bed-sitting room with four windows in a row and an open kitchen. It caught the sun between two and four-thirty. Then it sank into darkness. The rent was more than he had intended to pay; on the other hand, relieved as he was of any plans, the cost would surely hasten an end to all this and everything else. Then he recalled that he had left one of his notebooks back in the country. On a postcard, he sent his address to the Morands.

The routine he had made in the country he now adapted to the city. He had his coffee in the morning in one of the big old restaurants on Place Bellecour. He found an English bookstore, went to the library, forced himself to start reading again in French, following certain themes. He took long walks and prized certain views. At a point south of the city he rediscovered the most beautiful of all: the Rhone reflecting a colourless sky, framed by power pylons and hugged by muddy flats of gravel, all of it backed by a horizon of apartment blocks and two steel stacks with permanent gas flares. It was a view from his youth, a place where he had picnicked in a state of depression. Last, to his own amazement, adapted. One of his pleasures was a drink at midnight in Vieux Lyon or in the streets behind the university. He thought rarely of Nadine; life was once again simple.

He was happy for a while. The catalyst came when he forgot to pay his rent on time. The landlords were a couple – young and beautiful and unpleasant. They wanted him out for a friend who was cutting a documentary on the last of the Tsungut shamans and her male partner who did sculptures in silk stiffened with polyurethane. Fully aware that his lifespan was congruent with his savings, Last gambled everything by offering to pay a higher rent but the owners persisted in bringing a process for eviction. He resisted them with polite equanimity. Even they were impressed. If the dilemma awakened him, the conflict depressed him.

Around this time there was change at the Morands. A change which, nevertheless, neither of the elder Morands noticed; Nadine had become silent. Then, one evening, Madame Morand came across an application for the University of Lyon completed by her daughter. Wondering why on earth Nadine would give up the Sorbonne for something so second-rate, she fumed, preparing herself for another battle of wills.

Last, meanwhile, was on the verge of collapse. Shortly after the run-in with his landlords he had re-read his notes and saw chaos, the tailings of a mind desperate to occupy itself. The horrors he'd endured in Toronto during a spell of near-psychosis after he'd moved back to the street of his birth in a vain attempt to start anew – that, at least, had been something. But he had never faced Nothingness. Suddenly, his routines were empty. By the end of August he had lost his appetite; the mere sight of a child in Place Bellecour set him crying and he had to hurry back, averting his face to the walls. He forgot things; he would go back for his pen, leave again and go back for his notebook. He slept badly and after supper he would face a map of the city he had put on the wall, shut his eyes and place his finger on it.

Then he would walk there, no matter how far, and all the way back. Still, hours later he would lie in bed watching day emerge over the rooftops.

A week later, he stocked up on barbiturates, then changed his mind. Ending one's life with barbiturates left no statement; and in Toronto, long before, such an attempt had led to humiliation. The last minutes of horror in falling or drowning did not appeal to him, and if you cut your throat loss of blood could make you too weak to finish it properly. One afternoon, just as he was wondering how dangerous it would be to the other tenants to tape up the doors and windows and leave the gas oven open, the telephone rang. To his surprise it was not a telemarketer. Nadine was in Lyon and she had his notebook. She spoke as if it were only yesterday. There was a tone of intimacy, familiarity. He was silent. "Are you still there?" she said.

"Yeah, yeah. No. No. I'm sorry. I was just in the middle of something." She went on to explain: the comparative lit course offered by Lyon covered themes that the Sorbonne did not and she went to some lengths giving examples. These appeared to Last to be mere differences rather than refreshing alternatives and he was certain she had chosen provincial Lyon over the internationally renowned Sorbonne for obscure reasons of her own. Indeed, it occurred to him on further reflection that what she had done was completely self-destructive.

At seven that evening Nadine dropped by to give him his notebook. She was stunning, her clothes setting off her figure in a way that they had not in the country; her makeup subtle and striking. She must be meeting someone later, he thought. She showed a lot of interest in the apartment, its cost, its layout, its amenities. She updated him about the last months. Eventually, Last gave her a glass of wine. An ex-boyfriend had been harassing her, she went on. Her mother was impossible; when she'd heard that Nadine had applied to Lyon, she yanked the money from Nadine's bank account. Only by conspiring with her stepfather had she been able to enroll. Even though her stepfather was generous, he still seemed indifferent to the decisions she made about her life. He liked her but he didn't love her. It was getting late. Her considerable baggage was all over the floor near the door. Last wanted to go to sleep and wished she would go but she hadn't arranged for a hotel; she was supposed to stay with cousins of her mother but they were malicious and prying. Now she had an appointment in the morning. She asked Last if he had an alarm clock.

At four in the morning he vaguely watched her shoulder blades moving as she breathed, one of her feet lying back across his ankle. He was so sick and exhausted he couldn't sleep. She had three times, with considerable work, coaxed him into an erection and each time, he had, after a lot of effort, spent himself inside her. The third time was quite painful and his penis hurt. Her affection, despite what must have been a listless performance on Last's part, was surprising.

In the morning she left for her appointment, saying she'd be back at two that afternoon. He felt relief when the room was his own again; and later, because of her luggage, a sense of reassurance that she'd be back.

Over the next few days, Last began to sleep better. The problem now was that she kept him awake talking about her classes and professors and the other students, saying that it was all so provincial, nothing compared to the Sorbonne. He would drift off wondering what she had expected. By the end of the week the issue of her getting accommodation had failed to come up. On Saturday morning, as they sat in bed, she said, "I like you. You're a challenge." When he said nothing she went on, "At my parents' place I wanted to see if I could make you like me. I wanted to see if I could upset you. I mean, upset your routine, your calm. Like smashing an expensive vase. I also like you because you've had it with life. You have a perspective. You're so much against everything." It was true, but not particularly interesting in Last's opinion.

"You make me laugh," she said and giggled.

He would remember that it was raining when he gently explained to her that he had no work, had no intention of getting any and was living on a sum that was gradually dwindling and that, under the circumstances, it was uncertain whether he could ever love anyone. He also disliked society, constructed as it was so, frantically and painfully on hope and optimism. As he spoke, Nadine was reading a magazine and before he had finished she tossed the magazine on the sofa, stood up and told him the latest developments with an increasingly eccentric elderly prof in her sixties who looked like a transvestite. Then she suggested they go to a movie. They had supper and went out. Last had a strong sense that she understood him.

Still, he wondered if she really knew what she was doing and it took a while before he was convinced. One morning after sitting in a café, staring, he returned to find her on the bed in tears. His suspicion that she had finally realized the difficulties of being with Last, in other words, that she was normal, was immediately put to rest. In her hand was a faded, dusty copy of a literary quarterly.

"Is this it?" she asked, holding the cover up. He froze.

"Where did you find that? Who gave you permission?" he snapped, repeating it several times over, finally yelling. She had never seen him that way. Under the bed, she had found the poem that had almost launched a career, his first and last triumph. It was as good as anything she had read. Seventy-eight lines, six hundred and forty-two words, overpowering and ineffable. For Last, it was the stink of opening a grave. But he realized, after he had calmed down, that now she knew him. And that was how they began.

Over the following weeks a change occurred. It emerged from Last's growing conviction that it was Nadine's life that really had to be lived. Gradually, he began to cook, to help her with her computer, go shopping with her and talk to her about her family and friends, even when these things failed to interest him. They picnicked on the wasteland under the steel smokestacks. He surprised her by entertaining her school friends in an offhand way with odd stories from his youth. They found him a strange bird. Though he was often silent he turned out to have a skeptical bland charm that appealed to young men and women who had lost faith in achieving the least control over the world in which they lived. They were, needless to say, in the humanities. Nadine had her own life with them and came and left as she pleased, barely aware that Last found himself far less interesting than she or her friends found him. Nevertheless, she divined what still aroused him. When wearing a skirt without underwear, she would lounge on the sofa with one leg up and read or talk on the telephone to her friends in such a way that he could glimpse, up her skirt and through the shadow and hair, the pink invitation. This caused Last, in the armchair where he was slumped, to shift slightly.

Last had already come to appreciate her canny awareness of threads of mediocrity that still lurked in great writers; her individual yet impeccable taste in shoes; her earrings; her breasts; her self-discipline in matters of work, her nose. There was a charming negligence that came from confidence; soup stains in no way diminished her. A blotch of mustard on her cheek caused him to seize her and kiss her in a rare moment of spontaneity. The only thing that bored him was her fascination with suffering on which she expounded ceaselessly, intensely, her earrings swaying; for indeed suffering, which was no less surprising to Last than asphalt is to anyone else, bored him. There was, in the end, her extraordinary self-sufficiency, save in matters of sex for which Last somehow sufficed, he didn't know how.

The precise happiness of the pair is unimportant since it is impossible to know. What we can say is that an attractive and talented woman accepted the arrangement along with its certain end. What is also true is that one evening she leaned close to him and said, "I love you." A motorcycle buzzed away somewhere in the night. They were on the sofa in front of the television and Last was asleep as the tail credits for a literary show rolled. It was a re-run of an interview with Bukowski, who was by then deceased but was her latest passion. Last's eyes opened and she repeated it.

"Did you know that?" she said.

Last cleared this throat. "No."

The next day, upon returning from the bank, it occurred to Last that Nadine might want a formal, chivalrous courtship of the kind that many free, confident and self-sufficient women still seemed to crave. It might also be a good way for him to use the time allowed by the remaining 140,758 francs and 62 centimes. He bought her flowers, carefully and correctly chose her shoes, opened doors for her, made reservations at new restaurants, took her to odd places, squired her to the opera. He talked to her easily and patiently. For all he lacked, he had accumulated a lot of knowledge, most of it useless, which he was now able to apply at her whimsy.

That summer, they drove around the Lyonnais and Burgundy. Last wore a ragged olive tweed jacket, the last and only thing they fought about, and new prescription lenses that made his eyes look large and moist like a spaniel's. He would read aloud from a 1920s guidebook while she drove. (He was fascinated by what still existed, one of the last things that engaged him.) At this time he was feeling pains in his joints and was plagued by chest congestion but neither of them talked about it. In August and September Nadine had an affair with a fellow student, the son of a wealthy plastics manufacturer in Villeurbanne. Well before it ended, she told Last it was only physical and anyway she was soon revolted because the kid was spoiled. The kid was so heartbroken he attempted suicide. Last listened to her description of him with great interest and wondered if there was a way they could console him.

By the time Nadine was deep into her *maitrise*, Last was running a high fever. It was an unusually cold November; the wild storms that swept across Europe, hurling down trees, tearing the roofs even off city buildings, soon gave him pneumonia. In April he got it again and he was in and out of hospital. The doctors said his health was otherwise fine; it was just that he didn't have much fight. Nadine had fits of crying but to Last it was all a sort of progress.

In April they decided to get married since there was some question as to whether Last would expire before his visa. He had long had doubts about the idea of a matrimonial bond unto death but knew, at least, that this was likely to be short. Nadine's reasons were less practical: she wanted some sort of eternal bond and he had planned to be buried in a small cemetery below the smokestacks by the river in the wasteland where they had picnicked. The gas flares, he speculated, could be his eternal flame.

For a long time Nadine had put off asking him if he loved her. She had once sworn she would never ask him but now it seemed important. When she finally did she was on the way to getting her *maîtrise* with flying colours. He was in emergency in the Hôtel Dieu with an IV in his arm. Last himself never detested or despised Nadine, nor, apart from her obsession with suffering, was he bored by her. On the contrary, contempt and boredom, in Last's view, were the feelings most intensely associated with love. The proof of her love, if anything, lay in the fact that contempt and boredom were feelings she sometimes had for him. As for Last himself, he had missed her intensely on occasion, but with equal intensity he had missed his solitude. And so, instead of answering, he rolled over with a painful groan and rang for the nurse. The unspoken truth was that even if most people held that you had to love yourself in order to be loved by another, you could, in fact (and Last was the living proof, barely), be loved by another while not loving yourself.

Toward the end of May, Last had one of his few victories. The landlords, resigned to the fact that the law would not allow them a more interesting tenant, withdrew their case for eviction. The following day he died. He was fifty-one. Nadine was inconsolable. Their marriage certificate was still held up at the registry and she had to put herself down on Last's final record as a friend. She and her group commemorated his death with dinners and poetry readings. What they knew of his life had been quickly falsified into a legend of unrecognized genius. He was, it appeared, unforgettable. They celebrated the second anniversary of his death with a picnic on his grave, having invited a couple of male hitchhikers they had met on the way. With one of them Nadine subsequently fell in love. They broke up a couple of times and were married when she was thirty. It was a happy marriage.

On the fifth anniversary of Nadine and her husband, the two arrived at the cemetery with saucisson, camembert and some new Beaujolais. After finding, instead of a cemetery, an excavated waste, they made inquiries. The cemetery had been moved to put in a subdivision. The remains of those whose families could be contacted were carefully relocated to a new cemetery a short distance away. The remains of those who could not be identified had only that morning been put into a waste incinerator that now stood not far from the gas flares.

It was late in the day by the time Nadine and her husband opened the tablecloth in the upturned and empty cemetery and laid out the food. Smoke lay across the land and the sunset awash in violet fire. She gazed at the spectacular grey, vermilion and sulphurous west, the smoke and dust which was actually Last himself. Last, who finally consisted of that which he had been unable to express: the august grandeur of twilight, the twilight of his infancy on the street of his birth. And the nightmare of the street in maturity whose sun sank in sublime and lurid terror and expired in the ineffable peace of dusk. Nadine watched steadily, following him through the sky as he spread into the very polluted sunsets he had celebrated. Her old love was up there. He was up there and abiding, as he would be through all time.

ACKNOWLDEGMENTS

This book would not have been possible without the support of Norman Snider and his wisdom in selecting the stories; without the keen editorial eye of Barry Callaghan, and above all his insistence on continuity in a lot of very discontinuous material; nor without the tough and attentive editing of Nina Callaghan, and finally the impossible job of Michael Callaghan in putting it all together.

The stories first appeared as follows:

NEXT TO LAST: *Exile: The Literary Quarterly*, Vol. 29, No. 3, 2005

THE MAN: Winner of the Carter V Cooper Short Fiction Prize, with the 12 finalists appearing in the *CVC4 Anthology* and *Exile: The Literary Quarterly*, Vol. 38, No. 2, 2014

THROUGH THE SKY: Short listed for the Carter V Cooper Short Fiction Prize, and was among the 12 finalists to appear in the *CVC1 Anthology*

YOU MAY AS WELL COME DOWN: *The Antigonish Review*, Winter 2007

THAT'S ALL THERE IS: *The New Quarterly*, Autumn 2002, and the Oberon Press anthology *Best Canadian Stories 2003*

THE CHANGE: *The Antigonish Review*, Spring 2015

ELMIRA RAWLINSON: *The Antigonish Review*, Summer 2011

JOSIAH LOVE: *The Antigonish Review*, Autumn 2010

THE STREET: *The Antigonish Review*, Winter 2014

AFTER HISTORY: *The Fiddlehead*, Summer 2013

LAST: *Exile: The Literary Quarterly*, Vol. 28, No. 1, 2004

Hugh Graham has written for the *Toronto Star* and the *Walrus*, and his fiction has appeared in Canadian journals. He has twice been shortlisted for, and once won, the Carter V. Cooper $15,000 Short Fiction Award, those stories then appearing in the *CVC1*, *CVC4* and *CVC5* anthologies. He has published two books, with Exile Editions: *Ploughing the Seas* – a first-person account of CIA operations in northern Costa Rica during the war in Nicaragua – and *Where the Sun Don't Shine*, a gothic black comedy in dramatic form. The author lives in Toronto.